A second chance for true love…

Oh, god. Dare.

I couldn't breathe. Years of longing, dread, and grief filled me all at once. The ache in my chest that had started three years ago flared with new intensity. There was this gulf, this ocean of pain dividing us even though we stood mere feet apart. His jaw clenched as he looked at me, his deadblack gaze locked on mine.

There was only Dare in my world.

untamed 2

episode 2: out of control

jen meyers & victoria green

out
of
control

one

"*Ma chérie*, it would have been much quicker to take the metro, no?" Lucien huffed from behind me, most likely sweating to death in his tailored suit coat. And rightfully so. The walk to Montmartre—and my true destination, the artists in the square—was a hike.

"I told you I could meet you here," I said, my irritation rising. The metro was not an option for reasons I was not willing to share with him no matter how many times he whined. "You didn't have to walk with me. You didn't even have to come at all. I know where Place du Tertre is, Lucien. I told you that."

"I am gentleman," he said. "And you are new to Paris. It is my duty—and great pleasure—to show you around."

I could hear the slick smile on his face without even turning around, and fought the urge to shudder. It didn't matter how many times I told him I'd spent plenty of summers in Paris and that I knew the city well, or the fact that I spoke French fluently, he insisted on treating me like a helpless foreigner. As some damsel in distress for him to save.

Ugh.

I picked up my pace, suddenly regretting the tiny pink shorts I had on. They hugged my slender curves too perfectly, showed too much leg. Lucien had been way too appreciative.

Gentleman, my ass.

I made a mental note to be more careful about what I wore around him, though that was going to be a complete pain. Especially considering his disregard for personal boundaries.

Sharing an apartment with a man you didn't know—and an older one at that—was less than easy. But I hadn't had much choice. My decision to come to Paris had been a last-minute one, and Sabine had set me up in her friend's apartment while he was on an extended business trip to the States.

I'd known there would be a roommate—someone I'd be working with at the gallery—I just hadn't expected *Lucien*.

But life was never what you expected. Or what you wanted. It just stomped on your heart until you broke.

Or took pills.

Or drank yourself into oblivion.

Or fucked your brains out to stop yourself from thinking about—

NO. I was *not* going there. I couldn't think about him. Not without a lightning bolt of pain, not without the too-familiar vice tightening around my chest.

It had been three long years since I'd screwed everything up with Dare. Three years of trying to forget, and a single thought *still* hurt like a son of a bitch.

Fuck.

Paris HAD to get him out of my head. Out of my heart. Out of my freaking soul.

Paris and art—they had to be enough to obliterate his ghost.

Three years under my parents' thumbs hadn't done it. Three years of smiles forced through the haze of numbness. Three years of living someone else's life.

I couldn't do it anymore, and I'd finally realized *I* needed to do something about that.

"Why don't you go find some new artists for our Paris gallery?" Sabine had said six months ago when I'd started panicking about graduation and my impending incarceration in law school. "Get out of the country, be on your own, and find out if *this* is the life you really want, *chérie*."

My future had always been planned out with precision by my parents—political science at Columbia, straight to Harvard Law, and right into McKinley Enterprises. I'd gone along with it for as long as I could. Then something snapped.

"Trade in Harvard for art? Full time?"

The idea was shocking. Scary.

Exhilarating.

Paris. On my own. Discovering new up-and-coming artists. Maybe even gathering some for my future gallery.

Losing myself in the art world.

And maybe finding myself there, too.

"Do you really think I can do it?" I whispered, searching her intelligent hazel eyes.

Sabine cupped my chin in her hand and smiled. "I *know* you can. You have the eye—you always have. But *you* need to know that you can do it. And the only way for you to know is to try." She brushed my cheek with her thumb. "Take the summer. You have nothing to lose."

Nothing to lose? I had *everything* to lose. My whole life. The world I'd grown up in. My family, who would never understand. For the first time in three long, agonizing years, my heart was beating wildly as my mind and body hummed with excitement.

"You have to fly, *chérie*," Sabine said. "You have the wings, now it's time for you to use them. Remember…*vive la résistance?*"

I nodded. It felt like a lifetime ago.

Oui à la vie. Oui à l'amour. Oui à l'art.

Yes to life. Yes to love. Yes to art.

I could at least say yes to life and art.

But love? No. Been there, done that. Not ever doing it again.

After my talk with Sabine, I'd ripped up my acceptance letter to Harvard and bought a plane ticket to Paris. All on my own dime from the money I'd earned working at the gallery.

All without even telling my parents. At least not until I was up in the air and safely on my way. I couldn't risk them finding a way to stop me.

I needed this.

Like air.

And I knew I needed to have a blossoming career already in place when I finally revealed my plan for the future. Though I knew there was no chance of them approving, I had to make sure they couldn't fight me. Or, worse, sabotage my dreams.

So this was it. Paris. Art. The road to freedom. My one chance at life.

I deserved it. I'd fucking earned it with years of

blood, sweat, and tears.

Now, I paused at the base of Sacre Coeur, waiting for Lucien to catch up. The basilica's domes stretched up majestically toward the gorgeous blue sky above. It was breathtaking, and if I hadn't been so intent on getting started on my quest for new talent, I would have explored it right then and there.

But there was no time for that now. The first step toward my new life was waiting for me, and I could already feel the pull of the artists from where I stood.

When Lucien reached the top of the hill, he nodded at a little bench.

"Let's slow down and enjoy the view, *chérie*." He waved at the expanded vista of Paris below us—it was truly incredible—then lit a cigarette. Gross. "The artists can wait."

"But I can't," I said. "Take all the time you want, Lucien." With those words, I started toward Place du Tertre by myself. I was only moments away and could barely stand the anticipation. My entire body buzzed with a thrill I hadn't felt in a long time. It was like I'd needed to put an entire ocean between my parents and me in order to finally wake the fuck up.

I hadn't felt this good since—

Nope. Still wasn't going to think about him.

About us.

A few blocks over, the street opened to reveal the small artists' square already teeming with tourists. I slowly walked along the cobblestone street, taking it all in.

Color everywhere. The people. The languages. The art.

I'd entered my own personal nirvana as I started wandering amongst the crowds, exploring the various artists' displays. My heart pounded faster and louder with every new style and palette I encountered.

For the first time in years, I felt like I could actually see color again. Every shade and tone called out to me, warmed my gaze, seeped through my pores and into my skin.

It was so alive. And incredible. All of it. A beautiful chaos.

Up ahead, a couple of paintings caught my eye. Nudes in muted tones. But it was the style that stood out. Something about it struck a chord inside me. It felt eerily familiar and so very right. And I got that feeling I always had whenever I was in the presence of great art.

Hell, yes.

Without a doubt, I had found THE ONE.

There was a magnetic pull between my body and the art. I walked closer, my gaze glued to those paintings, my excitement growing with each step. My first artist discovery in Paris! The closer I got, the harder I shook. Chills washed over my skin. My breathing quickened. Honestly, I was pretty certain I was having some sort of religious experience. I could feel tears stinging the backs of my eyes.

Yes. I was in the right place. At the right time.

This was my Mecca—the reason I'd come to Paris.

Then I looked over to the artist, and froze.

Standing right in the middle of it all...was Dare.

two

Dare.

Oh, god. Dare.

The sight of him made my heart shatter all over again.

His eyes widened for just a moment, then he shut himself down, the hurt in them eclipsed by something far, far worse.

Distance. And cold uncaring.

I couldn't breathe. Years of longing, dread, and grief filled me all at once. The ache in my chest that had started three years ago flared with new intensity. There was this gulf, this ocean of pain dividing us even though we stood mere feet apart. His jaw clenched as he looked at me, his deadblack gaze locked on mine.

There was only Dare in my world at that moment.

I wanted to run to him, throw my arms around

his neck and crush my lips to his. I wanted to find out everything that had happened—where his family had gone, what he'd been doing...*how* he'd been doing. I wanted to say I was sorry, to demolish this distance and extinguish the hurt.

But all I could do was stand frozen in place and stare.

Someone bumped my shoulder, jostling me out of the trance. The smooth sound of French flowing between passersby pierced through. The artists' market came back into my consciousness, invading my senses with sounds and color and smells.

And the world began to move again.

Dare turned away from me and stepped behind his display, then said something to the artist next to him that I couldn't make out. I marveled at his paintings as I slowly walked toward him. Most of his work consisted of Paris landscapes, like so many of the other artists in this square. They were good—*great* even—though hardly a true demonstration of his incredible talent.

But he also had a handful of standout pieces that had caught my eye in the first place—the nudes. The color range of his palette hadn't changed much, but his style was more honed, more clearly his own. The light falling on the model's skin was warm, reminding me of the way the late afternoon light shone in his Brooklyn apartment all those years ago. And the more I looked at the paintings, the more familiar they seemed.

"What are you doing here?" His words were sharp, angry, and abrupt. I flinched in surprise. I hadn't realized he'd turned to glare at me.

My mouth felt dry and my brain sluggish as I struggled to come up with the right thing to say. Something that would smooth the harsh frown off his face, return the light to his eyes. Anything that would make him forgive me.

I'd spent so much time dreaming of this moment, hoping to see him again, to get the chance to explain, to make him understand and give me another chance. But all of my well-rehearsed speeches disappeared into the ether of my mind. What was left was as blank as a new canvas.

"I'm—" *Shit*. What was I? Anger rolled off him, crashing into me, rendering me stupid. "I'm so glad to see you, Dare." It was the truth, but from the look on his face it was the wrong thing to say.

"Really?" His eyes narrowed to dangerous, dark slits. I'd seen that look before. It was far from good. "Somehow I find that hard to believe. How can you be glad to see someone you don't know? Someone you've never seen before in your life?"

My words from three years ago were flung back at me. And they stung. Especially coming from Dare's mouth. I shook my head, but they cut into me regardless. I deserved this. I deserved his scorn. I'd done this. And all I wanted to do now—all I'd wanted to do every single day since it happened—was undo it.

Why didn't life have a rewind button?

I extended a hand out toward him, but he stepped back, keeping out of reach. Jesus. Was he really so disgusted by me that he flinched at the mere thought of my touch?

Yeah, I guess deserved that too.

"I'm sorry," I said, my voice shaking a little, tears threatening to spill. I forced them back and stepped closer. Lowering my voice, I said, "Just let me explain…"

"No, thanks."

"Dare, please…I just…" The look on his face stopped me cold. Okay. Now was clearly not the time. He was too angry. Even if I got the words out, he wouldn't be able to hear them. I knew this about him. But I didn't want to lose him again. I needed to keep him talking. "How did you end up in Paris?" I said as I waved my hand at his paintings. "Are you studying with someone here?"

He crossed his arms, the movement pulling his t-shirt taut against his hard chest. I knew the feel of those muscles so well, could feel the ghost of them under my fingers as I looked at him.

He considered me for a moment, then said, "Yes."

It was one word, but it was a start. I'd take anything I could get.

"That's wonderful. I can tell you've been working hard." I nodded toward the nudes. "Are those more recent?"

His gaze followed mine, then he glanced back at me, almost like he was trying to see if my question was sincere.

"Yeah," he finally said. "But the landscapes are what sell best on the street."

"They're good. Really good." I looked at him again to find him staring back at me, an unreadable expression on his face. "Your work stood out to me, which is why I stopped. I had no idea the paintings were yours. But they're the best I've seen in the square."

At those words, something changed in him. He didn't exactly smile, but the intensity of his glare lessened, and his frown diminished. Thank god! *Progress.*

"How long have you been in Paris?" I asked.

"Almost a year."

I wanted to say *Where did you go? I looked for you. I tried to find you.* But the words lodged in my throat.

All I could manage was, "Do you have an apartment here?"

He nodded. "Latin Quarter."

"Really?" My place was in the same district. That meant...maybe...MAYBE I'd get to see him again. Maybe he'd forgive me. Maybe... "Do you have a studio?"

"In my apartment."

"That's just...I'm really happy for you, Dare." I smiled at him. My *real* smile—not happy, but real. Pain still filled my chest, but there was something different about the sting this time. It was less sharp, more bittersweet.

His lips lifted at the corners just a bit, but his mouth immediately hardened when his gaze landed on something behind me.

"Ah, *chérie!*" Lucien said, coming up beside me and smelling like an ashtray. "I have found you." He put his meaty hand on my ass.

My entire body stiffened, stunned by the crude, abrupt gesture.

By the time I recovered enough to smack Lucien's hand away, Dare's face had become chiseled marble—cold and immobile. Hurt burned anew in his stony, dark eyes. He looked at me like he had no idea who I was, then turned and began to stalk away.

"No, wait!" I called after him, pushing past

Lucien. "It's not what you think!"

Dare turned and glared at me even as he kept walking.

"Don't, Reagan." He raised his hands, his eyes glass-hard. "Just fucking *don't.*"

And then he disappeared into the crowd.

three

Just like that, Dare was gone. Again.

I rushed around the square, searching for his tall frame, the black shirt he was wearing, the messy head of short hair...*nothing*.

No-*fucking*-thing.

Only laughing tourists, kissing lovers, and other people's happiness.

Mocking me.

With a heavy sigh and an even heavier heart, I gave up. It was useless. He was already gone, and even if I managed to locate him in the sea of tourists, there was no way in hell he would talk to me now.

I stormed away from Lucien, pushing my way through the people milling about. If I could've lost him in the crowd I would have. No such luck.

"Reagan! What is the matter?" He grabbed at the sleeve of my cropped sweater and I jerked my arm forward, picking up my pace.

"Go away!" I stopped short, and he slammed into me, wrapping his arms around me to keep us from falling. "Let go of me!" I pushed him away again and turned to glare at him.

"*Merde*," he said. *Shit*. His slicked-back hair was slightly disarrayed, and his dull gray eyes widened as he took in my face. "*Mon dieu!* You look like you breathe fire."

I shut my eyes and all I could see was Dare slipping out of my reach. Over and over again. And I fell apart, unable to hold on to my emotions any longer. Tears welled up in my eyes and spilled down my cheeks. A sob rose in my throat that I couldn't force back down no matter how much I wanted to. That black hole in my chest grew to a gaping vortex of pain.

For the first time in three years, I couldn't stop it, couldn't stuff the tears back down. The dam broke and overflowed right there on the street.

Lucien's eyebrows shot up in surprise, and his eyes darted around the square like he didn't know what to do. He managed to guide me over to a table at a café without touching me this time, then motioned for me to sit down as he ordered two coffees.

Which would've been sweet if I didn't hate coffee with a passion.

"Why the tears, *chérie?*" he said.

"That…was…Dare." I sobbed. "I…finally… found him…again…and now…he's…GONE."

"Oh, I see. He was your lover." Lucien smoothed back his hair in a well-practiced motion. He reached over and patted my hand. "Don't worry. I will help you forget this man, no?"

Um, NO. Not if he was thinking—

"One summer in Paris will cure you. This, I know." As he handed me a tissue, his smile seemed almost genuine. Like he was a concerned uncle. Well, one who wanted to get in my fucking pants.

I blotted my face and blew my nose as my mind began to work.

Maybe Lucien was right.

Not in the way he insinuated, of course. Because SHUDDER. But perhaps what I needed to do to get Dare out of my system was to have some sort of closure. The best way to do that was by seeing the person again, saying what you needed to say, and walking away. Right?

Though the thought of walking away from Dare just about killed me all over again.

If I was really going to do this, I was going to need something a lot stronger than a disgusting little cup of coffee.

My brain was buzzing just slightly, blurring around the edges thanks to those sweet little pick-me-ups I'd popped as soon as we'd gotten back to the apartment.

I needed it. I needed to not feel a single thing tonight.

I'd scoped out the hottest club in the Latin District, intent on not thinking about anything for one fucking night. The pills, the alcohol, and the blaring music would obliterate all unwelcome thoughts.

At least that was the plan.

When I'd come out of my room, Lucien had whistled low at my short, silver and blue vintage dress.

Thankfully, he wasn't invited.

He'd asked where I was going, but I just shrugged and said, "Out," grabbed my keys and walked out the door. I didn't want him coming along—I didn't want to spend the night prying his hands off me. Instead, I planned to forget Dare with someone who didn't skeeve me out because he was old and perverted. Someone safe. And, as always, forgettable.

The club was about a half block from the Seine.

Twinkling city lights shone out over the water, lighting up the river and my path toward pure oblivion. Although I was well aware that the Latin District spanned a large area, I couldn't help but wonder if Dare's apartment was nearby. How close was he right now?

I shook my head. *No.* This evening was supposed to be about getting my mind off of him...but I couldn't help it. Seeing him again today had brought everything back. All the memories I'd tried so hard to forget were fresh wounds again—the feel of his hands on my skin, his smell, the taste of him on my lips, the way his eyes crinkled at the edges when he laughed, the things his mouth did to me, his...

Stop it, stop it, stop it. *Focus.* I shook my head again and walked inside the club.

It was loud, the heavy bass thumping and blaring, the bar crowded with people—none of them Dare. I pushed my way through and ordered a drink just as Lucien slid onto the stool next to me.

My jaw dropped as I looked up at him with wide eyes.

What. The. Fuck?

"I thought you might want some company, no?" he said, and signaled to the bartender to bring him a shot like mine.

Fucking hell. The bastard had followed me.

I downed my shot and nodded for another. As the bartender refilled my glass, I caught a busty brunette giving Lucien the eye. With a deliberate point in her direction, I practically shoved him away from me. He shot the woman a quick smile and raised his glass, but then turned back to me.

"Go talk to her." I looked around the club for someone. Anyone. "I'm fine. You don't have to take care of me."

He nodded to the bartender for another round of drinks. "This is something I don't mind, *chérie*. I don't want you to feel sad about your lost lover." He reached over and stroked my hand once before I jerked it away. "You are much too beautiful to be down."

"I'm not down. The only place I'm going tonight is *up*," I said, forcing a laugh. I picked up my glass and drained it. The sharp sting of alcohol burned my lungs. *Good.* "I'm fine, Lucien. I appreciate your concern, but I'm going to go over there—" I pointed to the dance floor. "—to dance with THAT guy—" I picked out some random hottie. "—and have a fan-*fucking*-tastic night. You don't have to worry about me. At. All." I patted the bar on those last two words.

"How about you dance with me instead?" he asked, grabbing my hand. The feel of him holding onto my wrist made my heart hammer against my chest. The touch was too familiar. "We could have that good time together. Just you and me. Together."

I wrenched my hand free and slipped off the barstool.

It was okay. *I* was okay.

"No, thank you." I stepped away from him, suddenly needing to get away. As far away as I could. "I'm getting my happy on with *that* guy." I looked around. Wait. Where the hell had he gone? I blinked, then shook my head. Didn't matter. There were plenty of others. I glanced back at Lucien and pointed over to the brunette. "Go talk to her. She's waiting for you. Don't worry about me. I'll be fine."

He stared at me for a moment. "Are you sure?"

"I'm a grownup, Lucien." A screwed up, twenty-two-year-old kind of grownup. But at least I could find my way home without too much trouble. Or, better yet, into some random guy's bed.

Lucien shrugged. *"Si vous voulez."* *If that's what you want.*

It was. Sort of.

Because what I really wanted—the only thing in the world I wanted—was Dare.

A foot-aching number of songs later, I left behind my nameless, faceless dance partners to take a breather at the bar by myself. I could still feel Lucien watching me from where he sat with the brunette. His eyes had been burning into my skin all night long. No matter how hard I tried, I couldn't lose him in the crowd.

And now, to top it all off, his companion kept throwing nasty looks at me. I had no idea why as I'd made it clear I wanted nothing AT ALL to do with him, and was glad he was on the other side of the bar with *her*. She should have been sending me flowers. And chocolate. And drinks.

I looked down at my empty glass, then waved at the bartender.

More drinks. I needed more drinks.

More *everything*. I reached for the bottle of pills in my purse, but instead my fingers wrapped around a worn piece of paper. I knew what it was before I even pulled it out. It was the one thing that kept me sane—and broke my heart—every time I looked at it.

The phoenix Dare had drawn. The one he'd painted on me.

Four words written in his hand—*Two Parts. One*

Whole.

Our words.

"*Ça va?*" Someone tapped me on the shoulder.

The room swam when I turned my head toward him, and it took me a moment to bring him into focus. Tall, dark, and gorgeous. And not Dare. Of course it wasn't him. But this guy? He would do fine as the temporary distraction I so desperately sought.

As if reading my mind, the man held out a hand and nodded at the dance floor. "*Voulez-vous danser?*" he said, his voice low and lustful. *Do you want to dance?*

Sure. Why the hell not? Maybe he'd be the one to finally erase Dare from my mind.

God willing, *somebody* had to.

I'd been doing fine all night—GREAT actually—dancing with anyone and everyone, letting their hands roam places Sober Reagan would never have allowed, losing myself in the sensation of all the strangers, in the music, in the high. But now that I was thinking about him again…

Shit. I was on my way down.

And fast.

I shook my head, drained my drink, and stuffed the sketch back into my purse. Taking the guy's hand, I let him pull me out to the dance floor, glancing at Lucien as I went by. His eyes narrowed just slightly as we walked past, but then the brunette pressed her tits against him and said something in his ear that focused his attention back on her.

Good. Leave me the fuck alone. I wasn't his business. It gave me the creeps to have him watching me so intently.

The guy—Michon—pulled me close and started swaying to the music, his hands wandering all over my body. My back, my hips, my ass...I flinched when his fingers grazed my lips.

"*Si belle*," he said, gently sliding his hands into my hair. *So beautiful.*

I was drunk, yes, but the feel of him against me, of his foreign hands exploring me, the smell of his sweat—all combined to make me feel smothered, like I was suffocating. Suddenly the music was too loud, Michon too close, the club too hot.

God, I wasn't just coming down—I was plummeting.

I pushed against him, tried to step back, but he just pulled me close again.

"*C'est bon. Dansons*," he murmured in my ear. *It's okay. Let's dance.*

"No," I said and shoved him harder this time. He crashed into another couple and started cursing at me. But I didn't care. I needed out. I needed air.

I pushed my way through the crowd, looking back over my shoulder to make sure Michon wasn't coming. Thankfully, he was nowhere to be seen.

But then I saw Dare. He was here! Right across the room, his back to me. It was him—my vision might've been blurry, but it was him. I almost cried in relief as I squeezed through the crowd until I was directly behind him.

Taking a deep breath, I put my hand on his arm. "Dare?"

His head snapped up, and he turned to face me. Light blue eyes took me in, slowly, from head to toe and back up again. And then he smiled. *"Oui, chérie?"*

He wasn't Dare. Of course he wasn't Dare. God, what the hell was wrong with me?

My smile fell and I took a step back, bumping into someone else. Now that I looked at the guy in front of me, he didn't look anything like Dare. He was way too short and much too stocky.

My eyes blurred and the room swayed. I turned and pushed my way back to the exit, then out into the quiet dark of night. The crisp air felt good in my lungs as I started running toward the river. I just wanted to get back to the apartment so I could fall into the oblivion of sleep. If I couldn't achieve unconsciousness on my own, I'd dig right back into my little pharm bag for help.

"Reagan, *attendez!*" *Wait!* Lucien was hurrying out the door, pushing past a group of people on their way in. They yelled something at him but he didn't seem to notice.

I'd turned when he called out, and watched him rush over as the world swayed with me. His smile made me shiver as his gaze traveled slowly up the length of me to settle on my face. He studied my eyes and his grin got wider at whatever he saw there. Pain? Loneliness? Numbness from the drugs? Slipping his arm around my waist, he pulled me tight against his body.

"Our flat," he said in a disturbingly husky voice, "is this way, *ma petite.*" *My little love.* "Come. I take you home."

My skin crawled at the feel of his arm around my waist. I couldn't breathe. A loud, wild scream built up inside of me, starting at the base of my soul, threatening to burst forth from my lips. Panic raced through my veins, growing in strength, rising in intensity.

Darkness crowded my vision, and flashes of a familiar face flew through my mind.

I could feel his hands on me again, all over. Wine bottles out of reach. Everyone out of earshot. No one but the two of us.

I thrashed wildly, spinning away from him, trying to

claw my way out of the dark.

"Reagan! *Merde!* What is the matter with you?" Lucien's voice oozed through the fog in my mind as I fought to get away.

Wait. Lucien? I thought it was—

He let go and suddenly the street wavered in front of me as I pitched off balance. I grabbed for the side of the building, but missed, landing on my hands and knees. The sting on my palms blurred my sight with tears.

Lucien let out a string of curses, then shook his head and stalked away in a huff.

Finally, I could breathe again.

I was okay. I was in Paris. Outside. On my own.

I sat down on the sidewalk, the cold of the concrete seeping through the silky material of my dress, sending goosebumps shivering over my skin. Chills ran through me at what had just happened.

What *had* just happened? I breathed in, shaky, my mind trying to make sense of it all. I leaned back to rest against the wall of the building, but miscalculated the distance. Shit. The back of my head hit the sidewalk with a crack that reverberated through my entire body.

At impact, all the air left my lungs, and the shock of it—the insult added to injury—threw me over the edge. My head throbbed with every heartbeat as I lay there sobbing on the sidewalk, crumbling under the immense pressure of my past, present, and future.

Dare wanted nothing to do with me. There was no way I could go back to that apartment with Lucien. It was bad enough I had to work with him at La Période Bleue, but at least my job ensured that I'd be out on the streets most days scouting artists without him. But now I had nowhere to live. Just when I thought I'd succeeded at jumping over the first hurdle by leaving my parents behind, countless others presented themselves.

I didn't want to spend money on a hotel for the night, since for the first time in my life I had limited funds. And I couldn't—I WOULDN'T— ask my parents for help. Besides, I knew they would never help me anyway. Not without an ultimatum.

It felt like everything I was working for was already threatened, already teetering on the edge. If my plans to make a life for myself and escape the one my parents had mapped out for me failed, I would have nothing. Absolutely nothing.

It didn't help that I was lying on the sidewalk crying like some pathetic little girl.

God. I was stronger than this, wasn't I? I fucking had to be.

Okay, yeah, this night sucked, but I was NOT

going to admit defeat at the first little roadblock. I had to kick it down and dive back in headfirst. Go *all* in. I wanted a new life. *My* life. For that to happen, I needed to take my future into my own hands.

Right fucking now.

If I could just get up off the sidewalk, that is.

The cold from the concrete leached into my bones, and I started shivering. Warmth dripped down one of my shins. Great. I was bleeding. And my first thought was *no more skirts for me.*

I almost laughed. Almost. When I was six, I'd fallen off the jungle gym at the playground my nanny had snuck me onto, and scraped both knees. My mother hadn't even asked if I was hurt—all she cared about was that I would have Band-Aids sticking out from underneath my sundress. I'd had to wear long pants until the skin had completely healed. In July. In New York City.

Because *What in the world will people think, Reagan?* Everybody knew that McKinleys didn't bleed. They didn't cry. Nor ever got hurt. They were all just so fucking perfect.

Except, it turned out, one of us wasn't. She'd just pretended.

Footsteps rang out down the block as someone came toward me. Fuck, I had to get up. As soon as I lifted my head, the throbbing intensified and I squeezed my eyes shut with a groan.

Ugh. Even *that* hurt.

Thank god no one I knew was here to see me like th—

"Reagan?"

My breath hitched as I opened my eyes to Dare.

And this time, given the look on his face, I was fairly certain he wasn't a figment of my imagination.

four

God, he looked so amazing standing over me, running his hands through his dark hair.

His hands. How I missed the feel of those hands. If I could just reach out and—

He was talking to me, I realized. Blinking my eyes, I tried to focus on what he was saying.

"—doing here?" He looked around the deserted street. "Are you alone? Jesus, you're bleeding." Emotions warred across his face, and he looked like he was not quite sure of his next move. I watched him, mesmerized by his nearness, half wondering if I was hallucinating. But he smelled real—like leather, turpentine, and oil—and he felt very real as he scooped me up into his arms. "Come on," he said, his mouth warm against my ear. "We need to get you off the street."

I wrapped my arms around him and nestled my head into the crook of his neck. Running my hands over his back, I breathed a sigh of relief. Everything about him felt familiar and right. Like I was finally exactly where I was meant to be.

The walk to his flat was short, and too soon he'd put me down on the couch. He left the room, and I wondered if he'd be coming back. My head was pounding and the world was still spinning a little too fast.

He returned a few minutes later with a washcloth, some gauze, ointment, and tape. I tried to smile at him as he knelt down in front of me, but his face was hard and closed off. I couldn't bear the disappointment so I shut my eyes and leaned back against his couch, flinching when my skull connected with the cushion.

"Did you hit your head?" he asked. He'd moved up beside me, his voice next to my ear, his breath warming my skin as his hands slid under my neck to lift my head. I winced when his fingers brushed through my hair. "Sorry," he said, quietly. "There's no blood, so that's good. But you could have a concussion. Will you look at me for a moment?"

I turned and opened my eyes.

He was so close, his face mere inches away, worried eyes gazing into mine.

My pulse sped up, my breathing quickened. Everything I'd ever felt for him welled up inside of me as I stared into his dark gaze. It felt like no time had passed, that I hadn't done anything to send him away, that we were right back where we'd been.

Two parts. One whole.

His eyes dropped to my mouth. He inhaled sharply as my lips parted, aching for his kiss. All of my doubts melted away. I could do anything, *be* anything, if I had Dare in my life.

But when he looked at me again, his gaze hardened. The wall was back in place. He moved away and cleared his throat. "I think your head is fine."

Nothing about my head was fine right now.

I squeezed my eyes shut again, willing away the hot, stinging sensation of tears. Three years ago, I'd had to fight off butterflies around Dare. Now they were drowning in unshed tears.

I was such a fucking girl.

The washcloth was still warm when he gently pressed it to my knee, wiping the blood and dirt away.

"What happened?" he asked, his voice quiet.

What happened? EVERYTHING. The whole crappy night came rushing back and I had to fight to keep my composure.

Especially with him. He knew me so well—correction, *used to know me well*. I was not the same girl. It would be so easy to fall back into the familiar rhythm and just tell him everything. But he wasn't mine anymore. I didn't get to lay my problems on him.

"I…fell," I said, not even opening my eyes. I didn't know what he'd discover in them, and I didn't want to see the detachment on his face.

"You were sprawled on the sidewalk crying because you *fell?*"

I swallowed. "It's been a monumentally shitty day, okay? Can we just leave it at that?"

He was quiet for a few minutes as he spread ointment over the cuts and covered them with gauze, taping it in place.

When he lifted one of my hands in his, my breathing hitched. He was being so freaking gentle it was breaking my heart.

"So," he said as he cleaned the scrapes, "seeing me was really that bad, huh?"

My eyes flew open, and I shook my head. Which hurt. Fuck.

"No," I said, trying to smile through the pain. "That was the least shitty part of it."

The corners of his lips lifted, a ghost of a smile touching them. Which only made me smile for real. For a moment. Until I thought about the truly shitty part of my day.

"It's just…my roommate…he's giving me the

creeps. He watches me all the time, tries to put his hands on me—"

Dare's eyes narrowed. "The guy you were with earlier?"

"Yes." My voice came out shaking and breathy. "He followed me to the club tonight and was trying to take me home. I just...he reminds me of..."

"Of what?"

I shook my head. I wasn't going to think about it. Not now.

"I don't know what would have happened had I gone home."

Dare's jaw clenched and he blew out a slow breath as he wrapped my hand in gauze. Then he picked up the other hand and started cleaning it.

That sentence hung in the air between us, causing me to shudder at the memory of Lucien's hands on me, his eyes gliding over my body all evening long.

"Sabine set me up in the apartment. You remember Sabine?"

He nodded, his lips pressed tight. The hard lines of his face only made him more breathtakingly handsome. How had I forgotten how beautiful he was? How had I fooled myself into not remembering each and every angle to his face? I wanted to reach out and feel them under my fingers.

"So just tell her you can't stay there anymore." The way he said it sounded reasonable, but what would I tell her? That I didn't like the way Lucien looked at me? That he was being too friendly for my comfort? Aside from his overt sleaziness, nothing had technically happened. More importantly, I had nowhere to go.

I shook my head. "There's nothing to tell. It wasn't his fault that I hurt myself. I mean, yes, he'd grabbed hold of me, but he let go when I told him to. And I fell."

"He grabbed you?" Dare's gaze snapped to my face as his hands stilled around mine. His eyes were different after three years—there was no light. Or maybe that was just because he was with me. Little things stood out to me as I stared at him. His face was thinner, his jaw more tense. Everything about him seemed just a little...harder.

"It was nothing," I assured him.

"It doesn't sound like nothing," he said, focusing on my hand again so he could wrap it as he had the other. I watched him work, exhaustion overflowing and weighing me down.

"It's late," he said as soon as he'd finished.

"I know. I'll g—"

"Stay." He placed his hand on my arm to stop me from getting up, and my eyes widened in response to both the touch and his words. "It's late." He searched my face for a moment, as if waiting for my response, but I'd lost my voice. All I could do was nod.

Dare wanted me here?

"You hit your head," he said, as if reading my mind. "I just want to be sure you're okay."

Right. Well, his concern, at least, was something. At this point, I'd take anything I could.

He motioned for me to follow, leading the way down a short hall. The irony of the situation wasn't lost on me. Three years ago, the first REAL night we'd spent together had been in part due to his head injury. The one I'd caused.

Except that night had been perfect, sweet...back when I couldn't fathom sweetness. Tonight was just painfully bittersweet.

We stopped inside his bedroom. I stared at his bed—unmade, the sheets askew as if he'd wrestled with them all night long—while he walked over to his dresser and opened a drawer.

"You take the bed," he said. "I'll sleep on the couch."

"I can—"

"No." He stopped riffling through the clothes inside and turned to look at me. "You're hurt. You need the bed." He handed me a t-shirt and nodded toward the hall. "The bathroom is out there, the only door on the right."

"Thanks." I took the shirt, my fingers brushing his in the process.

Dare stiffened at my touch, his jaw tightening, liquid heat shooting into his eyes. He stared at my lips, and for a split second I thought he was going to reach for me. But then his fist clenched and he walked away. If that wasn't a clue that I wasn't entirely welcome...

I practically ran into the bathroom, only able to catch my breath once I was leaning against the firmly shut door. I knew I was a wreck even before I looked in the mirror, but the confirmation of the horror of my face was the last blow to my trampled self-esteem. Dark streaks ran down my cheeks from the black circles around my eyes, and my long hair was a tangled mess.

But it wasn't my outer appearance that bothered me as much as the mess inside my head that was clearly reflected in the watery depths of my gaze. For three years, I'd managed to stay cool, collected, unfeeling. At least on the outside. One day and one look at Dare and the reservoir had overflowed, allowing all those suppressed feelings to come spilling out.

Christ. I had to get a grip. Now.

I itched to take a shower and wash away the disastrous night, but with my knee and hands bandaged, that wasn't going to happen. I found a washcloth, dampened it, and scrubbed my face until it was clean. Then I used a comb to smooth out the tangles in my hair, wishing I had an elastic band to pull it back into a ponytail. When I looked in the mirror again, my honey-brown locks hung straight and silky down my back and although there was nothing I could do about the sorrow in my eyes, I looked more like the girl Dare used to know.

Reaching behind me, I tried to slip off my dress, but couldn't get it unzipped with my hands all wrapped up. So I opened up the bathroom door and peered out. I padded over to the bedroom and froze in the doorway as a drawer slammed.

Dare's back was to me, his arms reaching behind him to pull off his t-shirt. His muscles rippled as the material slid up and over his head, revealing the phoenix tattoo on his shoulder. The warm tan of his skin looked velvety smooth in the low light of the room and it took every ounce of self-control not to reach out and touch him.

No, I couldn't. He wasn't mine to touch anymore.

He picked up a clean white shirt, stiffening when he heard me shift in the doorway.

"I'll get out of your way," he started to say.

"Actually," I said, turning my back to him and pulling my hair over my shoulder, "I need your help, please. I can't undo it."

He paused and I stood completely still, waiting for him to make a move. Just when I thought he wouldn't, I heard him toss his shirt aside and cross over to me. His fingers grasped the zipper at the middle of my back, brushing my skin and sending a shiver through me. As he slid the zipper down, the dress slipped off my shoulders and fell to the floor, leaving me standing in front of Dare in nothing but my yellow lace panties.

He didn't speak, but I could feel his quickened breath as it grazed the bare skin on my neck. I imagined his gaze heating as he reached out for me, wanting to touch me as much as I needed to touch him. I wished I could just lean back into him and meld my body with his, back to hard front, skin to warm skin. A charged shock ran down my spine as I felt him close the distance between us, his hands hovering dangerously close to my waist. But then he cursed and moved away, jolting me back to the cold, harsh reality.

He wasn't mine to touch.

And I wasn't his to have.

So we were stuck in limbo—so close, yet much too far away.

I shook out the t-shirt he'd given me and quickly pulled it over my head. Then I lifted my hair out and let it fall down my back. When I turned to face Dare, he was staring at me, his expression one of pure torture.

Taking a deep, slow breath, he said, "Alright. I'll see you in the morning." He started to move forward, to go past me and out to the couch, when I panicked and reached out my hand to stop him.

"Would you…" I didn't want to be alone. I couldn't be alone. Not after Lucien and the memories. I didn't want to touch my pills tonight—not around Dare. But I would never get to sleep on my own otherwise.

His brow furrowed. "What?"

"Would you stay with me?" When his eyes narrowed and he started to shake his head, I barreled on. "Not because I want to…you know…I just…" My breaths were coming in quick little pants as I tried to keep my panic at a manageable level. "I can't be alone tonight. Not after…everything."

Not after YOU.

He searched my face as if the answer was written in my eyes.

"Please, Dare? I promise—"

He nodded once, but didn't say anything, so I

shuffled over to the bed, so freaking grateful I couldn't even speak. I climbed under the covers, sliding all the way over so there'd be plenty of room for him to lie down without having to touch me. I turned my back to him and tucked the pillow under my head. I'd taken a couple of aspirin from his medicine cabinet, and the pounding in my head was already starting to wane.

Dare pulled the covers up on his side of the bed, then lay on top of them. The feel of him next to me—not even touching me, just his mere presence—put my whole body at ease. I felt myself relax like I hadn't been able to in ages. My exhausted mind and body felt weighed down after the events of the day, and I drifted off to sleep with the sounds and smell of Dare all around me.

five

I woke in the middle of the night snuggled up next to Dare, his arm wrapped tightly around my waist. For a brief, insane moment, I thought I'd imagined the whole thing—that the past three years had simply been a bad dream and we were back in his apartment in Brooklyn. And this whole fucking nightmare was just a warning from my subconscious to save me from my own self-destructive stupidity.

But instead of the sounds of New York City, I could hear the streets of Paris below. Soft melodious French drifted in through the open window and I remembered, with no small amount of embarrassment and horror, the details of the previous evening.

Dare's hand was warm on my stomach, keeping me securely fastened to him as his long legs entwined with mine. The whole length of him along my back set my senses on high alert. With each lungful of air he took, I could feel every hard, tight muscle in his chest expand and contract. His soft, warm breath caressed the back of my neck, bringing with it the sweet, minty smell of toothpaste and something more familiar.

Something all Dare.

Being here in his arms again, even though I knew he would never have touched me like this consciously, made me miss him even more. It brought all that I'd lost front and center, giving fresh intensity to the gaping hole in my heart. I couldn't stop the silent tears from slipping down my face as I lay there listening to him breathe, the pain of all that I'd never have again nearly splitting me in two.

I'd been so fucking stupid. How could I have let him go?

Why hadn't I been stronger? Why didn't I fight tooth and nail for us?

If anyone was worth sacrificing everything for, it was Dare.

I slowly turned my head so that I could glimpse his face. Three years had changed him. Made him rougher around the edges, even in deep sleep. But he was still Dare—arresting beauty of an art masterpiece and striking hardness of a sculpture.

My Dare.

How painful those two tiny words were to even think now that I was right in the middle of everything I so desperately needed and wanted in my life...and all that I no longer had. Not having him was the worst feeling in the world, like trying to exist without a vital organ.

My Dare wasn't mine anymore.

I turned away again, and he shifted in place, his hand tightening around me. I reached down and slowly lifted it up. I stared at it for a moment, studying the length and thickness of his fingers, the lines of his palm. I'd always liked those hands, was easily mesmerized by them—especially when he sketched—and had once known the feel of them so well.

The faint smell of turpentine still clung to his skin as I brought his hand closer to my face and pressed my lips against his palm, breathing him in. At my touch he drew in a quick breath. I could feel his shoulders stiffen, his whole body going rigid.

Shit, shit, shit. I had not meant to wake him; I'd just wanted to bask in his nearness. I froze, anticipating the loss that was surely coming.

Was he going to pull away? Would he get up and move to the couch?

To my surprise, Dare didn't remove his hand. He stayed as still as me, like he was waiting for my next move. So I opened my lips and slid my tongue along his palm, tasting him. He exhaled sharply and groaned. As I pressed another kiss to his hand, I could feel him hardening against my lower back. So I kissed him again. And again.

He moved then, leaning up on one arm and pulling my shoulder toward him so I was facing up. My heart raced and my head spun at the sight of him looking down at me. I opened my mouth to speak, but no sound came out. I was too afraid to say anything, too scared to break the spell. He just kept looking at me, searching my face, hungry want pulsing so clear in his eyes—the same want I felt deep within my soul.

Slowly, he reached out and trailed his fingers over my cheekbones and along my jawline as if making sure they were exactly how he remembered them. When he traced my lips, I parted them. His eyes were fixated on my mouth, his fingers just skimming the rim, driving me wild. The tip of his index finger slid toward my tongue and I closed my lips around it, sucking it deep into my mouth.

He grunted and lifted his gaze, his eyes scorching mine. Slipping his finger out of my mouth, he stared at my lips for a moment, then leaned down and crushed his mouth to mine with so much unbridled desire I saw stars behind my eyes.

And I met him. Just as eagerly.

His hand gripped my chin, keeping me locked to him while his tongue consumed me. Dare kissed me as if he were dying of thirst and I was life-giving water. He drank me in—hard and fast—and then drank some more.

And I drank him. Just as greedily.

He left my lips, kissed down my jawline to my neck, sending shivers over my whole body—the body that was waking up in places that had been dormant since the day he'd left. Pulses of pleasure shot through me, heating my skin and making me wet with want.

Still not saying a single word, he grabbed hold of the t-shirt I was wearing and ripped it right down the middle, exposing me to him. His mouth found my breasts, licked and kissed around them, getting maddeningly closer and closer to my nipples. When he finally claimed them, sucking, nipping, making me ache for him, I cried out and arched my back, rubbing my throbbing core against him.

I tugged on his shirt, needing to feel his skin against mine, needing to feel *all* of him. He yanked it over his head and threw it to the floor. Overwhelmed by the sight of him, I ran my hands over his chest and stomach, caressing every ridge of hard muscle. He watched me as I explored him, his eyes turning darker still. Feeling the familiarity of him under my hands was almost too much to handle. I lifted my hips to press against him again, and his gaze shot straight to my panties.

He sucked in a sharp breath and ran a hand down my stomach, his fingers skimming the lace as he leaned down and took one nipple into his mouth, and then the other, licking and teasing them into tight buds. Leaving my breasts, he kissed and bit his way down the center of my chest and stomach, then reached down with his other hand to pull my underwear off, tossing it down next to his shirt.

His kisses grew rougher and fiercer as he made his way along my inner thigh, lingered right above my ache without touching me, and trailed a path of kisses to the other. Then he did it again. And again. Almost like he was punishing me by purposefully depriving me of him. The next time he paused at my throbbing center, I wove my fingers into his dark hair and lifted myself up to his mouth. His tongue flicked out and licked me. Once. Twice. Three times. Then he lowered himself down, took me into his warm, wet mouth, and sucked.

And I became completely lost, totally absorbed

by him. The rhythmic feel of his mouth on my clit sent electric bursts spreading out from my core, building up to a feverish charge that pulsed through my body. I was almost at the moment of bursting into flames when he pulled his mouth away, leaving me a raw, writhing mess, aching with so much want.

I looked up at him, pleading with my eyes for the release only he could give, but he'd gotten off the bed to pull a condom out of the bedside table. He slid out of his shorts, his erection so strained and huge it caused a whole new throb within me. Every muscle on his body was its own masterful work of art, so beautifully sculpted he almost seemed unreal. As unreal as what was happening right now in this room.

A small sigh of relief escaped me when he returned to my side. I didn't want to be separated from him. Ever again. Dare was my answer to a three-year-long call, a fire that ignited feelings and emotions after a lifetime of cold, harsh nothingness. He wreaked havoc on my body, but soothed my mind and healed my soul.

I needed him. So fucking badly. And I wanted to make sure he knew it.

Before he had a chance to unwrap the condom, I reached for him, filling my hands with his hardness, running my lips over the hot, smooth velvet of his skin. Even in the dimness I could see his eyes flash dangerously, but he didn't resist, allowed me to slide my tongue over him and take him into my mouth.

God, I'd forgotten how good he felt, how perfect he was.

I took him deeper into me, all the while keeping my gaze locked on his. His jaw tightened and his hands fisted at his sides as if trying to resist the urge to grip my hair and agitate the bump on my head. I rewarded his concern by licking and sucking faster, taking in as much of him as I could. His head fell back and he groaned, his hips starting to move with me.

But then he stopped suddenly, gripped my shoulders, digging his fingers in, and pushed me back onto the pillows.

My heart sank at the brutality, feeling the rejection to the depth of my soul until I heard the sound of ripping foil. One glance at Dare erased every worry and kicked my pulse up ten notches. He'd opened the condom packet with his teeth and rolled it on. Before I had a chance to make a move, he spread my legs wide and buried his hard length in me without hesitation. I cried out from both the pleasure and pain of being this close, this tight, this full of Dare.

He took hold of my hips with both hands and

thrust into me over and over again, like a man possessed by need, completely out of control. I gasped at the feel of him, so hard and hot and deep inside of me.

Rolling his hips he pumped slowly once, twice, then groaned and began moving faster and harder like he couldn't help his need for me, like he was functioning on raw, primal instinct. His eyes burned into me as he took me higher and higher, increasing the intensity of his movements.

It was almost as if all the caged emotions he held behind that deep, fathomless gaze erupted and engulfed him, shooting out of his body and into mine. In this moment, Dare possessed every part of me—all my senses and thoughts, every bit of my happiness and pain.

And he knew it.

His body melded with mine, his eyes imprisoned me, his mouth consumed me, his scent filled my nostrils, his sounds flooded my ears. Every thrust brought me closer and closer to the edge, until my body was tingling all over and about to burst forth with a vengeance that was three long years overdue.

Sensing my oncoming orgasm, Dare's fingers threaded into my hair, his pace quickening to match the beat of my own sprinting heart. My hands gripped his back and my nails dug into his

skin as he brought his mouth down on mine
again, crushing and impatient, our tongues tasting
each other as we climaxed together.

Little lights burst like fireworks on the backs of
my eyelids as the orgasm rocked through me. My
whole body tingled. From head to toe and
everywhere in between. I hadn't felt this alive in
so long. And I'd NEVER been so wholly claimed
and devoured by another person the way Dare
consumed me.

Spent, he collapsed on top of me, breathing
heavy, his body glistening with a slight sheen of
sweat in the soft light that filtered through the
window. I wrapped my arms and legs around him,
not wanting to let go, but knowing that I'd
eventually have to.

Our breathing calmed and Dare shifted. I
reluctantly released him and he pushed himself
up, pausing above me. I looked up to find his
dark eyes boring into mine.

There it was again, that expression on his face
that I didn't know how to interpret. It was filled
with years of unspoken... *everything*.

Anger. Hurt. Tension. Desire.

Neither of us spoke. Maybe, like me, he feared
that words could break this maddening trance we
were in. He got up, walked across the room to
dispose of the condom, then came back and slid

under the covers. I wasn't sure which way to turn, whether he'd want to sleep alone on his side of the bed, but then he reached for me, pulling me into the crook of his body, skin to skin, and holding me tight against him.

I squeezed my eyes shut, but the tears slid out again.

Silent. Scared. And grateful.

When I finally relaxed into Dare again, we both drifted off to sleep.

six

The sun woke me, shining in through the window, filling Dare's room with bright morning light. We hadn't moved the rest of the night, and were still cuddled up together, his body so warm and alive against mine. I squeezed his arm, hugging it close to my chest, relishing the feel of his nakedness.

And I sighed, happy—truly happy for the first time in what felt like forever.

I was whole again here with Dare. Right. Complete.

He stirred behind me and I nestled in a little closer.

But then he stiffened. And my heart plummeted, fleeing my body entirely.

Without a single word, Dare pulled his arm out from around me and rolled away, sitting up at the edge of the bed. I turned to watch as he rubbed his hands over his face, then leaned down to pick up his jeans and quickly slid them on. He didn't even spare a single glance my way.

I closed my eyes and shoved the pain in my now-empty chest away. Of course it was this way. Why would I expect anything else?

"You should get dressed and go," he said from the doorway, one arm up on the frame, his back to me. "I have to work."

I sat up, clutching the sheet to my body, feeling way too naked in the light of day. God. I hadn't thought this through last night. At all. Staying here, waking up with him. Leaving.

I didn't want to leave. But I couldn't stay.

He didn't want me anymore.

Fuck.

Dare didn't turn around, like he couldn't even bear the sight of me in his bed, and after a moment he started to walk away.

"But…" I said, not quite believing these words were coming out of my mouth. How many guys had said this to me? Karma was a vengeful bitch. "But…what about last night?" It was all I could do to not cringe. I was so fucking pathetic.

He turned and looked at me then, and immediately wished he hadn't. His face was emotionless, his eyes stony and uncaring.

"Last night?" He shook his head. "Last night

was a mistake. It won't happen again."

The harsh words hit dead center, and I could feel the anger rise in my chest. I scrambled off the bed, the sheet barely wrapped around me, fuming.

"You know what? I didn't ask for last night. I didn't ask for your help. I'll be out of your way in about five minutes. *Three*," I said as I snatched my dress and panties up off the floor, "if you get out of the fucking doorway and let me get to the bathroom."

Of course, I had no idea where I was going to go. I'd have to go back to the apartment to get my stuff—god willing Lucien would be long gone to work by then—and I'd need a place to put it all. A hostel perhaps until I could find something more permanent.

Fuck, this day was looking to be even worse than yesterday.

If that were even possible.

I stalked toward Dare and he glared for a moment before moving aside. Brushing past him, I almost lost my grip on the sheet, but grasped it tighter, pulling it around me with my other hand.

As I was about to storm into the bathroom, he spoke. "There's an apartment in this building."

"What?" I whipped around to face him again.

"It's available," he said, almost reluctantly. Because he didn't want to piss me off or because he didn't want me living in his building? I didn't know, and frankly, I didn't care. "I could talk to the owner and get you in. You need a new place to stay, right?"

"I don't need your fucking charity, Dare. I can figure things out on my own."

I rushed into the bathroom and tried to slam the door as hard as I could, but he moved in after me and held out his hand to stop it midway.

"It's not charity." His voice floated through the slightly ajar door, low and tight. "It's the right thing, and you know it. You can't live with that creep. You need a new place and there's one here. Take it, Reagan. I won't offer again." Releasing the door, he turned and walked away.

And left me all alone.

Again.

When I pushed open the door to La Période Bleue that afternoon, Lucien's crooked smirk greeted me as if nothing at all had happened last night.

"*Bonjour, chérie!* I did not see you this morning. Are you alright?" He actually had the audacity to look concerned. I put my palm on his chest and stepped out of reach as he leaned forward to try to press his cheek to mine in a *bise* greeting. His eyes widened for just a moment before narrowing at the insult.

Whatever. Douchebag.

"*Je vais déménager,*" I said. *I'm moving out.* "I just thought you should know."

His face hardened slightly, and his eyes flicked to the door behind me as it opened.

"*Bonjour!*" he called out to the young couple who'd walked in. "*Un moment.*" *Just a moment.* Then he focused on me again, stepped forward and slid his fingers around my elbow, pulling me with him toward the office. "We should talk about—"

Yanking my arm from his grasp, I glared at him. "It's done. Leave me alone." I nodded toward the customers. "Go. You have work, and so do I. I'm going to scout. I'll be back when I find something suitable for the gallery."

Then I turned and walked away, ignoring his shocked expression. I didn't have to make nice with Lucien. That wasn't what I was here for. He didn't deserve it anyway.

Out on the street I took a deep breath, the scents of late spring flowers filling my lungs. Feeling just a little freer again, I started walking. The farther I got from the gallery and Lucien, the better I felt and the easier I could breathe.

Of course, this was just one problem solved. There were many more to go.

But what was that saying? One day at a time?

Damn it. I wanted it all accomplished in one day.

But I didn't live in that kind of world anymore.

That was my parents' world—as long as you were willing to pay enough, you could just snap your fingers and get a list of wishes fulfilled in a single day. Any problem could be solved in the time it took to sign a check. Hell, with my father's money, he could even make the problems vanish. Like *that*.

He'd even done it with things I didn't necessarily consider problems.

As if on cue, the pocket of my jean jacket shuddered as my phone vibrated. I didn't even bother looking at it. I knew what awaited me. There were a couple of texts from Archer—the closest friend I had, but most of the buzzing was due to the countless voicemails I hadn't listened to yet—every single one from my parents. I'd left a parting note for them that explained my intentions for the summer, packed my bags, and gotten into a car to the airport. No goodbyes. Nothing.

They never would have let me leave if I'd told them what I was doing, that I was choosing my own path for once. They would have found a way to blackmail me into staying. They always did.

Right now, the only way to truly make it was to do it on my own, using my own money. And it looked like I was going to have to do this the hard way—one single, slow day at a time.

"Cecily Annabelle Edwards," a woman's sharp voice cut into my thoughts and I looked up to see a mother and her three children coming out of a fenced-in schoolyard. The two older ones crossed the sidewalk in front of me and marched straight into the Bentley waiting at the curb, but the smallest girl had frozen at the sound of her name. The woman gripped her arm and pulled, causing the child's face to twist in pain.

"A lady does not ever sit on the floor, Cecily." She spat out the words as she dragged the child toward the open car door, the little blonde girl's perfectly polished Mary Janes scraping the pavement as she tried to keep up. "What will people think? Only the homeless sit on the ground."

"I was just playing, Mama."

"I couldn't care less what you were doing. Your father and I do not pay good money for you to attend a prestigious American school and embarrass us by acting like some uncivilized degenerate. When will you learn?" She pushed the girl into the car, stepped in herself, and shut the door.

Chills ran down my back. The woman had been coiffed to perfection. Her clothes were expensive and immaculate. Her tone cold and harsh. She was my mother. A carbon copy.

I watched the car pull out into traffic, saw the little girl's face—heartbroken, ashamed—as it went by. She looked at me with big doe eyes and I smiled sadly, hoping she'd know that someday it would be okay.

Someday. Yes.

But someday could be a lifetime away.

After a full afternoon of traversing Paris and taking note of a few possibilities for Sabine's gallery, my feet ached and my bruised knees were sore.

And I still had to unpack all my stuff in my new apartment.

When I'd come out of the bathroom that morning, cooled off and calmer, I'd found Dare in the kitchen drinking a cup of coffee. He just looked at me as I stood in the doorway, not speaking, not offering me anything. Not even a cup of tea.

Once upon a time he would have had a steaming mug waiting for me.

Obviously, the fairy tale had ended. Without the

happily ever after. And I was stuck standing in the doorway still pissed, but needing his help.

Fuck. Me.

"Okay," I'd said.

He raised an eyebrow but didn't say anything.

"I want the apartment." What I really meant was, *I NEED the apartment.* But part of me didn't want to admit just how desperate I was for Dare's help. Not after the way he'd acted. I crossed my arms and noticed his gaze flick to my chest. Which just made me think of last night and spawn a whole new set of knots in my stomach. I did not want to be thinking about last night. Ever, if I could help it. "So who do I need to talk to?"

He put his cup down on the counter and motioned for me to follow.

We left his apartment, and walked down the stairs to the ground floor. He knocked on the door closest to the front entrance of the building. A crooked old woman opened it, her face lighting up at the sight of Dare. She immediately reached for his shoulders as he leaned down to press his cheek to hers—first on the right, then the left— and spoke to her in fluid French.

Holy shit. Dare was speaking French? When did that happen?

The language sounded delicious on his lips, the words sliding smoothly out of his mouth and surrounding me in the vestibule. I wanted to breathe them in, soak them up. God, it was getting me hot just listening to him.

And that was exactly what was not supposed to be happening. I remembered his words clearly. *Mistake*, he'd said. *Won't happen again.*

Just like that my head was clear, my mind feeling the hard edge of anger.

Won't happen again. You bet your sweet ass it won't happen again.

Dare gestured at me, and the woman looked over with so much warmth in her eyes I almost had to take a step back.

"*Bonjour*," she said, "*Je m'appelle Anais.*" I'm *Anais.* Then she took my arm and led me back up the stairs to the door across from Dare's.

My eyes flew to his, but he was purposefully not looking at me. Live right across from him? And if the layout of this place was anything like his, it meant we'd be sharing a wall, too.

My heart hammered in my chest and my palms began to sweat. I didn't know if I could do this. Be *this* close to him. Because, come on, this was a little much. I'd figured seeing him again would give me the closure that everyone always boasts about, but living right next to him was more than I'd bargained for. Much more. When he'd said there was a place in the building, I was thinking *somewhere else*. Another floor. Waaaay down the hall. Definitely not THIS close.

Oblivious to my panic, Anais unlocked the door and led me through the apartment, her silvery-white waves catching the morning light spilling through the windows. The place was fully furnished with a tan, overstuffed couch, a few Kandinsky prints on the walls, a kitchen that would get no use since I couldn't cook, and a tiny little bathroom just like Dare's. The bedroom was airy and bright.

It was so fucking perfect.

I had to take it.

I mean, obviously I *had* to take it because I couldn't live with Lucien and I had nowhere else to go, but I HAD to take it.

As for Dare being right next door? Well, I guess I'd have to ignore that. And hopefully eventually learn to live with it.

He'd gone back to his apartment while Anais and I settled on rent—she'd agreed to just below my monthly maximum, thank god. Once I'd received my set of keys, I'd gone back to Lucien's, packed up my few things, and brought them all over. I'd just dumped them in the living room, changed my clothes and left.

But now I was back in my new apartment— tired, sore, in need of a shower and food.

And ready to get my life back on track.

Again.

Three hours later, I was lying alone in the dark, desperately trying not to think about the feel of Dare's hands roaming over me, his tongue teasing my most sensitive places. His touch was imprinted on my skin. Every time I closed my eyes I was back in his bed, writhing in pleasure, throbbing with want.

Every time I opened them, I was alone.

So fucking alone.

Sleep was never going to come at this rate, so I got up and pulled out my bag of tricks. A couple of pills worth of relaxation and half a bottle of wine to wash them down still didn't erase Dare from my mind. If anything, I was feeling even more riled up. I could practically see him hovering above me, his eyes glinting in the darkness so full of raw need and pure greed.

The fact that I knew he was right next door, just on the other side of the wall, only made it that much worse.

Last night had been a trip to heaven, only to be plunged straight down into the fiery pits of hell this morning. I wasn't sure if Dare had wanted me or if he'd simply wanted to punish me. Maybe both. The way he kissed me, touched me, fucked me…

God. I had no thoughts that did not relate to him. And sex.

Okay, I could do this. I could last the twenty minutes it was going to take for the pills to kick in. I glanced over at the clock. Nineteen and a half minutes.

My hand slid to my stomach…

Dare.

…and my fingers traveled lower…

Dare, Dare, Dare.

…slipping down the front of my pajama shorts.

Fuck.

I needed a distraction. And maybe another drink. Wrapping a robe around me, I slipped out of my room and padded barefoot across the thickly carpeted living area. Halfway to the kitchen, I stopped, the scene outside of the window catching my eye. Paris was lit up, twinkling like a magical land just waiting to be explored.

For what felt like an eternity, I gazed at the bright lights and the streets I knew so well. I loved this city so much. I'd always wanted to live here, and now I was. Sure, so much was screwed up in my life at the moment, but I was living in *Paris.* Some things were right.

My head was starting to swim in that delightful way it always did when the pills and booze kicked in. My whole body relaxed into a dreamy heaviness, and I felt a little dizzy. Good. I was on the verge of blessed oblivion.

Time to lie down.

I tried to walk around the side table to get back to my room, but I missed a few steps and ended up bumping into a lamp. It teetered and tipped, but I was way too fascinated to do anything about it except watch as it fell in slow motion, landing on the floor with a fantastic, colorful crash.

Oh, wow. Now the room was spinning. I stepped over the broken pieces and crawled onto the couch. It was so soft and squishy, and just right for snuggling up and falling right to sleep.

Just as my head hit the cushions and my eyes were closing, there was a loud knock on the door.

Dare said, "Reagan?"

I looked at the door and waved, too tired to form words.

He knocked again. Louder. "Are you okay? REAGAN?!"

I wanted to tell him everything was fine, but my mouth wouldn't work, my eyes didn't want to stay open any longer. Where the fuck had this feeling been ten minutes ago when I'd needed it?

There was a bang and the door flew open.

Dare's tall frame filled the doorway, outlined by the light spilling in from the hallway. He looked around the room, took in the smashed lamp and said, "What the fuck is going on over here? Are you alright?"

Then he was next to me, squatting down so that we were face-to-face. I could feel his warm breath on my skin, so I opened my eyes and reached out to touch his cheek.

"You have such a nice face," I said with a soft laugh.

His eyes hardened. "Jesus. Are you...*high?*"

I nodded. Then shook my head at the look on his face. "Couldn't sleep. Just needed a little help to relax." I pointed out the window. "I love Paris. Don't you love Paris?"

"Yeah." He stared at me, looking like he wanted to say something more, but my eyes started to close again and he sighed. I felt his arms slip under my legs and behind my back, and then I was lifted up into the sky. I wrapped my arms around his neck, leaned my head against his shoulder, and breathed him in.

He carried me into my bedroom, gently laying me down on the bed. I snuggled into the covers and felt the pull of the earth throughout my entire body.

Everything was a jumble in my mind, getting

mixed up and moved around. My thoughts were hazy, my entire body loose and warm.

I drifted off to sleep, my mind laced with Dare.

seven

Light barely leaked into the room when I woke the next morning. I inhaled deeply, trying to get rid of the fuzz in my brain. Blinking a few times, I looked around. The curtains were drawn, which was strange because I always left them open, and the layout of the bedroom didn't seem quite right.

For a moment, I was certain I'd be doomed to a Parisian walk of shame, though I had no recollection of seeking that out last night. But I'd moved yesterday, I remembered. This was my new place.

Last night I'd unpacked and—

"So you're finally awake, Princess."

My gaze flew to the other side of the room where Dare sat in a deep green stuffed chair. His hair was a mess, his eyes bloodshot, and he was rolling his shoulders and neck with a wince as if he'd spent the entire night in that chair.

Shit. *Had* he been here all night?

"What…?" I started to say as I sat up, but he cut me off.

"What the FUCK are you thinking?" He sat forward, his elbows on his knees, and glared at me. "Are you fucking insane?"

I shook my head, trying to remember what had happened last night, but came up blank. Sure, the Ambien had made me loopy, but what had I done to make him so freaking angry?

"How can you still be taking those damn pills?" My little orange bottle was in his hand—and my heart stopped. Part of me was ashamed and the other part was panicked that he'd take them. He shook the vial at me before chucking it across the room. Then he picked up a wine bottle from the floor. "AND with alcohol? Are you REALLY this fucking stupid, Reagan?"

For a moment I wondered if he was going to throw that, too. But then his words sunk in.

My jaw clenched and I narrowed my eyes at him. He had no right calling me stupid.

No fucking right.

"Look—"

"No, YOU look, Reagan. You almost DIED three years ago. Do you get that? The last time I saw you, you were lying in a hospital bed looking like shit and fucking lucky to still be breathing after all the crap you'd swallowed. And…" He broke off, and started pacing the room as if he was searching for the right words but couldn't find them. Then he stopped and his face lost its hard edge. It was softened with so much pain I almost gasped. "...it almost *killed* me. If you had died..." He shook his head, and was all hard lines again. "And you're still using? Are you fucking kidding me? You're smarter than this." Then he stopped and stared at me again, fire burning in his eyes. "At least the Reagan I knew was."

He was not going to throw that in my face. Fuck that.

I tried to scramble out of the bed, but the sheets were tangled around my legs. The more I pulled on them, the angrier I got. By the time I'd ripped the covers free and my feet hit the floor, I was fuming.

"The Reagan *you* knew? You mean REE?" I laughed. Actually laughed. Without joy, without humor. It sounded as hollow and cold as my mother's voice. "Oh, that's RICH, Dare. She's LONG gone. The Reagan you knew doesn't exist anymore. She died when you left."

"Me?!" His eyebrows shot up into his hairline as he jabbed himself in the chest. "You're blaming *me?* You didn't want me. You made your choice. Loud and clear."

"And I was *wrong!*" I threw my hands up in the

air, my heart hammering against my ribcage. God, I wanted to throttle him SO badly. "Jesus, I was in the fucking hospital surrounded by my family, my father's finger hovering above his phone, ready to destroy you if I said anything. What did you expect me to do? I was trying to protect you!"

"No, you're right," Dare said, his eyes blazing. "Why would I expect you to fight for me like I would have fought for you?"

"Fight for me?" My voice rose in pitch and volume. "You would have fought for me? Was that before or AFTER you didn't return any of my messages? Was that before or AFTER you left without saying goodbye? Without telling me where you'd gone?"

He stopped then. Searched my face as the truth of what had happened dawned on him.

"I called you," I said. "I texted you. For WEEKS. I snuck out to your gallery show to see you. To *tell* you." Tears were stinging the backs of my eyes but I pushed them back and drew in a deep breath. "To be with you, go wherever you were going."

Dare stood frozen in place, his brow furrowed, his eyes burning into mine. And then he closed the distance between us, took my face in his hands and crushed his mouth to mine.

And I was alive again. Electricity ricocheted

through my body, making me tingle from head to toe. I opened my lips, tasting him hungrily as my hands grabbed fistfuls of his white t-shirt to pull him to me, anger and desire equally fueling my movements.

He seemed to be operating on a similar cocktail of fury and need as his hands slid into my hair, his tongue roughly tangling with mine. An ache started to pulse between my legs and expanded into a throbbing need that coursed into every part of my body, igniting my blood until I was certain fire burned through my veins. I bit down on his lip, pulling it between my teeth and let go of his shirt to dig my fingers into his back. I opened my legs wanting to feel him against my hot, aching core, and he gripped my ass, lifting my legs to wrap around him.

His skin was hot and smooth, his muscles hard under my touch. He kissed me rough and hard, angrily taking everything I was more than willing to give, possessing every part of me. He pushed us forward until my back banged up against the wall, pressing me as tight against him as I could be.

And still it wasn't enough. For him or me.

I tugged at his hair and rocked my hips forward and was immediately rewarded with the hard length of him pressing against me. I moaned at the feel of him, my panties instantly soaked.

In this moment, I wanted him more than I'd ever wanted anything in my life.

But there was a loud knock out in the hallway, and he suddenly stopped and pulled away. His head tilted toward the door, listening. Someone called out his name.

A woman.

Dare put me down and backed away, groaning as he ran his fingers through his hair.

"Shit," he said under his breath and wiped his mouth against the back of his hand as if he were wiping off my kiss. Looking down at me, his chest heaving, he shook his head. "I can't do this with you, Reagan. I *won't.*"

Then he turned and walked out of the room.

I stood staring after him, listening to my door open and then click closed. In between, I heard the delighted sound of a woman greeting him.

Mon amour, she called him.

My love.

My legs gave out and I slid down the wall to the floor, but my heart kept going, dropping out of my body and down until it was deep underground where I could not go to retrieve it.

Why was I doing this to myself?

And why in fuck's name couldn't I resist him? He was like the worst kind of addiction to the

most amazing drug I'd ever had. I knew I needed
to kick this habit if I was going to get on with my
life...I just didn't know if I could.

Or if I wanted to.

eight

The next two weeks dragged by, punctuated only by my few, tense conversations with Lucien about the artists I was finding, and a growing procession of women going in and out of Dare's apartment every night after I got home.

Every. Fucking. Night.

I crossed paths with them on the stairs or heard them laughing out in the hallway as I scoped out artists online. I even ran into Dare and the bimbo-of-the-day when I went out to pick up dinner a couple of times.

He was everywhere.

On my mind, in the building, on the street.

Everywhere but in my life.

And it hurt. Draining-the-life-out-of-me pain.

Which made me think that I pretty much sucked at this closure thing. Either that, or it was a total crock of shit.

But tonight, strangely, all was quiet. No women, no sounds at all from his apartment. For once, I felt like I could relax and drop my guard.

I shut my laptop, plugged it in, and left it on the desk. Then I went out to the kitchen to get a glass of wine.

And that was when the lights went out.

Everything went out.

The apartment was pitched into darkness, and I froze.

Too dark. It was too dark. No light came in from the streets, no moonlight shone through the windows. The world around me was just black.

Like a cold, dark cellar.

My heart started hammering, and I drew in a deep breath. Deep breaths were supposed to help you calm down, right? But after a couple of them I was pretty sure that advice was a crock of shit too because I wasn't feeling calm AT ALL. In fact, my heart was trying to pound its way out of my chest as waves of panic flooded me, threatening to drown me.

Hands. I could feel his hands.

I swung my arm around behind me, knocking the wine bottle to the floor with a crash.

No one was here. No one was here.

My pulse took flight. I struggled to breathe as my lungs screamed for air. With every quick, strained breath, it felt like no oxygen entered my body and I became more lightheaded.

No one here, no one here, no one here.

Of course no one was here. I was alone in my apartment in Paris. At least I thought I was. And I needed to get outside where I could breathe, before I started screaming.

Holding my hands out in front of me, I stumbled out of the kitchen, feeling for the wall, hurrying toward the door. I wasn't being careful—I didn't have *time* to be careful. I needed out.

He whispered something in my ear.

Goosebumps prickled my skin. I whipped around but couldn't see anything.

I took a step, tripped, and started falling, my arms flailing out in front of me. I landed hard and something crashed to the floor next to me.

It was him. He was here.

The screams came out with a will of their own as I squeezed my eyes shut and kicked at nothing. I clawed my way toward the exit in the pitch black, scrabbled for the doorknob, flung the door open and rushed into the equally dark hallway.

And crashed right into him.

Oh, god. His arms came around me, holding me still, trapping me in the dark.

With him.

I thrashed around, kicking, trying to break free, but he held me tight. My screams turned to sobs as I realized I couldn't get away.

Again.

But I wasn't going to stop fighting.

"Reagan, it's me! Calm down. You're okay," Dare said. "Ow! Fuck that hurt."

Dare?! Not—

"REAGAN!" he yelled, gently shaking my shoulders. "You're safe. I've got you."

I inhaled…and smelled art—oil paint, charcoal, and graphite. It really was Dare.

I was in his arms. Safe.

"Look," he said. There was a little click and his face was lit up. "It's me. You're okay."

I stared at him for a long, silent moment, my eyes open wide, my wild pulse slowing down as my vision filled with him.

Finally, I could breathe again. I looked around the hallway—his door was open and I could see faint amber light flickering off the walls. Candles. He'd lit candles.

I was okay. It had all just been my imagination. Thank god.

My hands started shaking, and the rest of my body followed suit.

"Hey." Dare lifted my chin, his brow crinkling in concern. "Jesus. That really freaked you out.

You okay?"

I nodded, glancing back at my apartment door and the darkness inside. I did NOT want to go back in there by myself. I'd spend the entire night outside on the street until the power came back on if I had to, but I was not going back in there. Not until there was light.

As if reading my mind, Dare said, "Come on," and gently pulled me into his apartment.

Candles flickered from the center of the coffee table and the kitchen counter. Dare guided me over to the couch, sat me down, then went into the kitchen. He came back a moment later with a bottle of tequila and two shot glasses. Without saying a word, he poured and handed me one. I downed it immediately.

The burn made my eyes water and I could feel warmth spreading out through my system as if the heat of the alcohol was already flowing in my veins. Dare held up the bottle in a silent offer of more, but I shook my head.

One was enough. For once. Plus, I could already feel its calming effects. If I was back in my apartment, I'd be reaching for my pills. I glanced up at Dare, wondering if he knew that. If he knew just how much I wanted them right now. How badly I needed them.

He was staring at me intensely, the answer to

my question etched in the furrow of his brow.

"So…?" he said. "The dark still bothers you."

"Something like that." I pulled my knees up to my chest and wrapped my arms around them. I was not going to tell him about it. I wasn't going to tell anyone. Ever again. The two people I'd told—my parents—had failed me.

No. Not just failed. They'd *betrayed* me. In the worst possible way.

"Do you want to talk—"

"No." *Please, no.*

I couldn't even think about it. No need to awaken seven-year-old demons right now.

A muscle in Dare's jaw popped. "Reagan, obviously there's something—"

"It's none of your concern," I said, my cheeks flushing. Why was he pushing this? Why was he pretending to care? He didn't want me. "You've made that perfectly clear."

"Reagan."

"Let's just not tonight, okay?"

He poured himself another shot, drank it and put his glass down on the table before he answered. "Fine."

I sighed. A strained silence stretched between us. Finally, I broke it because I couldn't stand it anymore. "How's your family? Where are they now?"

Dare leaned back in his chair and looked at me from across the table. "California. We moved there from New York three years ago to get as far away as possible."

Whoa. Punch to the gut.

"From me?" I said, my voice quiet. Had he really hated me that much?

"From my dad," he said. "Not everything is about you, Princess."

I looked at him hard. "But *that* was. You were getting far away from me, too."

He worked his jaw, clenching and releasing it a couple of times before he nodded.

"How's your mom?" I said.

"Same. She's…mom."

"What about Dax and Dalia?"

At the mention of their names he lit up. A small smile touched his lips as his gaze fell to his hands. His face filled with warmth that I hadn't seen in a really long time.

God, I'd missed it so much, and I hadn't even realized it until I saw it again. But that kind of light only came with belonging. He clearly felt it with his brother and sister, which just accentuated the cold, dead hole in my life where that feeling should have been.

I belonged nowhere, with no one. I'd broken from my family—where I'd never belonged in the first place—and was now on my own, more alone than I'd ever been. I had Sabine, of course, cheering me on from New York, but other than that? Archer. We'd talked a couple of times since I'd gotten here, but he just kept trying to convince me to come back, to go to law school and live the life I didn't want. He didn't understand.

But Dare? He had everything I wanted.

He WAS everything I wanted.

And I was everything he didn't want. God, I was so fucked.

"They're good," he said, bringing my attention back to him. "Dax got a football scholarship to UCLA and Dalia's working in L.A. and studying acting."

"Acting? That's great." I could definitely see Dalia on stage or screen, that kind of role seemed like the exact right fit for her. It had been so long since I'd let myself think about the twins—it felt bittersweet to hear about them now. "I'm so happy to hear things are going well for them."

Dare opened his mouth, then shut it again as if he was trying to decide whether to say something. After a couple of false starts, he finally said, "They're coming to visit."

"Really?" I couldn't keep the smile from my face or the happiness from flooding my heart. I knew I shouldn't be so excited about it because who knew how they felt about me after all this time, but I couldn't help it. "When?"

"In a little less than three weeks."

"That's just so…wow." I stared at him, chewing on my bottom lip. "I'd really like to see them when they come. If that's okay. I mean, I'm sure you guys have plans. Are you taking them places? Traveling?"

"No." He shook his head, and another breathtaking smile lifted the corners of his lips. "I…uhh…actually have a show coming up."

My mouth hung open and I just gaped at him for a full three seconds of stunned silence.

"A show? At a gallery here in Paris?" I let go of my knees, put my feet on the floor and leaned forward. "Are you kidding me?" I wanted to throw myself into his arms, but instead stayed firmly put. "That's AMAZING. Why didn't you tell me? Where is it? Which gallery? Are they good? Have you checked them out? When is the opening?"

"Whoa!" Dare's broad chest vibrated with deep laughter, the sound of it warming my insides. "Slow down, Reagan."

His eyes locked onto mine and we just stared at each other for a moment, so many unspoken words and feelings still hanging between us.

Too much.

My heart ached, but I couldn't look away. I was simultaneously thrilled for him and despondent for me. Where he had everything falling into place, I had everything falling apart.

We were separated by so much more than three years and a few feet. Even though I was living in his world now, we were not in the same place at the same time.

And it killed me. Especially since there was nothing I could do about the distance.

The ball was in Dare's court now, but he wasn't even interested in playing the game.

nine

Galerie Yves Robert faced the street, its full wall
of windows towering above me as I paused
outside to catch my breath. It had been a long
walk to get here, and for once I was wishing the
cab drivers weren't on strike—I'd be tempted to
splurge on a ride home. After my heart calmed, I
pulled open the door and walked inside the empty
space.

Dare had assured me he knew what he was
doing and had refused my offers to check the
place out for him. He'd said it was a reputable
gallery, and from what Sabine had told me when I
talked to her earlier, he was right. In fact, it was
more than reputable; it was one of the finest
galleries in Paris. And the fact that Dare had
gotten a show here was remarkable—they were
known for their exclusivity. Sabine had gushed
when I'd told her.

"Wilde...he has done very well for himself." I could hear her beaming even over the phone and practically saw her nodding her dark head. "I am wishing he was showing at La Période Bleue, of course, that you had scooped him up before Yves. But," she'd said, "I showed his work first. Next time I am in Paris, I will be sure to mention this to Yves."

Sabine hadn't been exaggerating about this gallery, either. It was exquisitely laid out. I explored the room, slowly taking in the paintings on the walls, trying to decide whether I would have seen any promise in the artist they were currently exhibiting. The work was good. Very mainstream. The paintings had a strong style, but they didn't fully grab me. Didn't squeeze my heart and refuse to let go like great art always did.

Of course, not all art appealed to all people. But as a future gallery owner, I would need to be able to pick out the art that would stand out and please the masses. Realizing that I probably would not have chosen this artist for a solo show made me question myself.

Was I really cut out for this? Would I find success? I so desperately wanted answers that I snapped a few pictures so I could discuss them with Sabine and find out whether she saw the same promise in the artist that this gallery had.

All the while, I couldn't help but think that Dare's work was so much better and more compelling. It had been even before I knew he was the artist of all those nudes back in his Brooklyn studio.

There was something about his pieces that kept me rooted in place, made me want to look and look, and then look some more until the art and I became one. I noticed something different every time—the shape of a shadow, the way he created a feeling of calm, the fact that I could almost hear, taste, smell, and touch the moment he'd captured. His work surpassed the visual and delved into dimensions very few artists ever reached.

I imagined these walls covered with Dare's work and got goosebumps at the thought. His paintings were going to shine in the bright white space, and I couldn't wait to witness his success. I only wished I could be a part of it. If only a tiny one.

Voices murmured behind the wall where I stood, and a moment later a door opened and swung toward me, blocking me from sight.

"But what about all of my landscapes?" Dare was saying as I stepped closer to the wall. Shit. I wasn't supposed to be here. He was going to be pissed if he saw me. My eyes stayed on the art, but my ears were fully focused on his words.

"Those sell really well out on the street, I'm sure they'll—"

"Galerie Yves Robert is not the street, Dare. The owners are most interested in your unique nudes and want more of those for the show."

"I showed you all I have right now." Dare's voice was a low growl. "I haven't been happy with any of my models lately. The last few I tried to work with just weren't right. And by the time I find the one I want, it'll be too late to have any more pieces ready. Finding the right subject is a process, Jacques." He clenched his fists, the muscles of his arms tightening.

The man shook his head. "If you cannot provide more, then we'll have to reschedule."

"But I have family flying in from the States for this. You can't change the date on me."

"I can," Jacques said, "and I will if I have to. Our clients come first and we need to give them what they want...whether it's from you or from someone else. Bring us more nudes."

Then he turned and retreated into his office, pulling the door closed behind him, taking away my hiding space.

I stood frozen in place as Dare stared at me with blazing, narrowed eyes. His jaw tightened and his lips thinned into an angry line. He didn't say a word, just spun on his heel and stalked toward the door.

Fuck.

"Dare, wait! Please!"

He ignored me and stormed down the street, forcing me to run to catch up.

"Dare!" I grabbed his arm.

When he spun around to look at me, his expression darkened and his eyes turned to stone, and I immediately wished I hadn't touched him.

He glanced down at my fingers that were still wrapped around his arm and I pulled my hand back, breaking the connection between us.

"Please," I said, breathing hard, stalling for time. I had no idea how I was going to explain myself. Just when it seemed like we'd made a little progress, I had to go fuck it all up again.

"What the hell were you doing there?" His words were tinged with both fire and ice. "I told you to stay out of it. I can do this on my own."

"I just—I was so excited for your show and then I talked to Sabine about it—"

"You were checking up on me? Are you fucking kidding me?"

"No, it's not that," I said, panicking. "I mean, yes, I was. Sort of—" His face darkened. "But not the way you think. I was just telling her the good news. That's all. She had lots of good things to say about Yves Robert."

"Un-*fucking*-believable. I never should have told

you. I knew you wouldn't be able to keep your nose out of it." He shook his head, ran his hands through his hair. "I assume you heard everything?"

I bit my lip. "I can help you."

His eyes narrowed. "Yeah? How?" There was a dark challenge in his voice.

My mind raced. La Période Bleue! I could get him a show there. And Sabine would crow about it. She could rub it in Yves' face and I could do the same to Lucien. It would be a coup! My shining moment—except I was supposed to be doing this for Dare, not myself. Though if it benefitted us both...

"I can set up a show for you at La Période Bleue in a few weeks," I told him. "So you have enough time—"

Dare shook his head. "Dax and Dalia already have their plane tickets. I can't change the date. And I don't need you pulling strings for me, Reagan. I've been doing this on my own for a while now. I don't need your help."

God, he was SO—

"I *know*," I said, my hands fisting at my sides, my words coming out through clenched teeth. "You've done amazing, Dare. I'm only trying to help because you're obviously in a bind and you can't do *everything* on your own. Sometimes you actually need other people, you impossibly frustrating,   too-talented-for-your-own-good, fucking prima donna."

His eyes widened, then narrowed. Oh shit. It was like I was TRYING to sabotage myself. What he needed was time and—

"A model!" I shouted, causing the people walking by to glance at me in surprise. I lowered my voice and said more calmly, "I can be your model."

He stared at me for a moment, unmoving, studying my face as if he wanted to know whether I was actually serious. Obviously, I was one hundred and ten percent serious.

"No. I don't think so." He turned, but I clutched his arm again and didn't let go this time.

"Dare, I heard what the gallery owner said. You need more work. You need a model—"

"I need a *nude* model." There was that razor-sharp challenge again, and now it was starting to piss me off.

"I *know*." I raised an eyebrow and crossed my arms over my chest. "You used to draw me, right? And it worked. Very, very well from what I remember. So if you need—"

"I don't *need* you, Reagan," he said, cutting me off. "I'll find some girl to pose for me."

"But why look for *some* girl when you can have

me? The *right* girl."

I was playing with fire. I knew it. But I didn't care. The muscles in his jaw twitched as he stared at me, his eyes dark and fathomless. There was no caring in there—no hint of it—just ice-cold contempt.

Good god, I'd really pissed him off this time. I almost lost my nerve, but lifted my chin and held my ground.

I wanted this.

I wanted him.

And I would do whatever it took.

"Say yes, Dare. Say you need me." My words were filled with so much double-meaning I was no longer sure if I was trying to convince him or myself.

After what felt like forever, he nodded—just barely. Then he jerked his head toward the next block and started walking.

"You start now."

ten

"Right now?" I nearly tripped over the curb as I ran after him.

He turned to glare at me, walking at a gracefully fast pace only someone his height could manage. "You wanted to do this. I need to get started right now if I'm going to keep my show. Are you in or not?"

I nodded. "Yeah. I am. I'm in."

All in.

When I looked at Dare's back as he led the way, the butterflies inside my stomach started up again. I'd fucking done it. I'd guaranteed myself time with him.

When we got to the corner, I turned to walk back toward the apartment, but Dare stopped me.

"No," he said. "We're taking the metro, Princess."

"But," I said, my pulse pounding at the thought,

"we can walk. It's not that far."

It was REALLY far, but there was no way I could go below ground. Just the thought made me shudder.

"I need to get started NOW," he said. "I don't have time to waste strolling through the streets of Paris just because you don't want to take public transportation." He glared at me, the ultimatum clear on his face. *Do this or go home.* He knew how I felt about underground spaces, though I'd never told him why.

"You'll have to set up, right?" My mind was racing. There had to be some way around this. "I'll meet you there. I'll walk fast. I'll run."

He looked down at my sandals, and raised an eyebrow at me.

"Okay, I'll *walk*—but really REALLY fast. It won't take me long, I promise." I glanced at the stairs leading into the darkness. I couldn't. I couldn't go down there.

He shook his head. "The metro." And he took a step down. "If you want in the game," Dare said, not even looking at me anymore as he headed underground, "you gotta play by my rules."

Fuck. Me.

I was sweaty and shaking by the time we got to our stop. I'd kept my eyes closed, fists clenched on my thighs the entire horrible ride. Dare sat next to me, pressing his body against mine, possibly in an effort to help, but nothing could soothe the panic in my mind and body. It had been seven long years since the last time I'd delved into an underground space.

Ever since—no. No, no...*stop*.

I wouldn't think about that now. I wouldn't think about it EVER.

I dashed up the stairs to street level, gulping in air like I'd been suffocating. In a way, I had.

Dare followed close behind, concern marring his handsome features. It was even worse than when the power had gone out. He'd never seen me this bad—no one had, not for a long time. And there was nothing he could do.

He searched my face. "Jesus, Reagan. Are you okay?"

I shook my head. Then nodded.

"What just happened?" He reached out to touch my cheek, but stopped himself. "I mean, what...I don't even know what the hell to ask you."

"I wasn't kidding when I told you I don't like...places like that." I closed my eyes, but a couple of traitorous tears slipped out. I took some deep breaths, trying to force the panic back down.

"It's not because I'm being spoiled. It's...just—"

"I'm sorry," he said. "I wouldn't have asked you to do that if I'd known how bad it really was."

"You didn't know." He had no way of knowing.

"Do you want to talk about it?"

I shook my head, silently pleading with him to just drop it.

He took a step toward me, and reached out to touch my arm, his hand stroking up and down, his fingers brushing my skin gently and with purpose. His calmness seeped into my body, and my wild pulse and the tremors slowly subsided. That simple gesture felt so good, so right. I closed my eyes, basking in the warmth of his touch, and breathed him in.

Color. God, Dare still smelled like color.

He was intoxicating.

I could've stood like that forever, but he cleared his throat and stepped back. I couldn't look directly at him for fear the eyes gazing back at me would still be cold and distant. He stood there for a moment longer before taking my hand in his, linking our fingers together, and leading the way to our building.

Although he didn't speak a single word, something had shifted in his touch—almost like he'd let go of the rigid armor of anger he'd been ensconced in all this time. I breathed a sigh of relief. Maybe taking the metro had been worth it after all.

Once inside his apartment, Dare threw his keys on a little table by the door, then headed down the hall in the opposite direction of his bedroom. He led me to a bright room. His studio.

Oh, god. His studio.

It had been so long since I'd seen him work, my knees felt a little weak just from being in proximity to the canvases and paints. He had a platform set up for a model, and I tried not think about the other naked women he'd spent time drawing, painting…touching.

The thought hurt so much I actually winced as it pierced my mind.

Dare pulled out a blank canvas and propped it on his easel. Then he picked out a few brushes and started sorting through paints. He glanced up at me, his face wary. He nodded toward the other end of the hall.

"You can get undressed in the bathroom," he said. "There's a clean robe behind the door." Then he went back to his paints.

I nodded and turned to walk down the hall.

It always took him at least fifteen minutes to set up his stuff, so I decided to take a quick shower. I felt disgusting and sweaty after the metro, and knew I'd feel more comfortable if I wasn't worried that I smelled like panic and pain. I stripped off my clothes and piled my hair up on my head to keep it out of the water.

A few minutes later, I toweled off and wrapped the robe around me. It was long and silky, obviously something he kept for models. And all the women who came and went, regardless of whether they posed for him.

I tied the robe tightly, then walked back down the hall to his studio. He was almost set up, his palette ready, his brushes in place, a cup of coffee in his hand.

The canvas in front of him was a big, white, blank space full of possibilities. I wished my life had been like that—defined only by the limits of my imagination—and not filled by my parents like a perfect paint-by-number picture.

But now it could be. I was in Paris, after all, trying to free up my life's canvas by erasing some of the lines, painting over them, making my own. This—being here with Dare, helping him—felt like a step in the right direction.

He nodded over toward the platform where a futon mattress lay with a chocolate brown blanket covering it. My hands started shaking and I swallowed hard, suddenly filled with nervous energy. Which was ridiculous because this was *Dare*. I trusted him. Once upon a time I'd wake up to him sketching my naked form after a night in his bed. He knew me. He'd seen everything I had—very recently, in fact.

There was nothing to be nervous about.

And yet there was everything to be nervous about. This felt like one of those pivotal moments in my life when everything was on the line. If I screwed it up, my life would go off track, be colorless again.

I had no idea why I felt this way, why this seemed so huge, but it did.

I glanced at a little table right next to the mattress—there was a hot, fresh cup of tea sitting on it. Oh, my god. He'd made me tea. That was just so—

"You ready?" he asked quietly.

I turned away from the tea, and nodded. Maybe everything was going to be okay.

"Yeah," I said, and waved my hand at the platform. "How do you want me?"

Dare didn't answer right away, so I looked up to find him staring at me with a quiet storm brewing behind his gaze. He swallowed hard before speaking. "A simple reclining pose. However you're comfortable."

Turning away from him, I stepped up onto the platform, pulled the ends of the tie at my waist, and let the robe slip to the floor. Then I took out the elastic from my hair and shook out the long strands, letting them cascade all the way down my back.

I lay down on my side, my back to him. "Is this okay?" I asked, my voice coming out too breathy. I felt more naked than I ever had in my whole life.

He didn't answer, so I glanced over my shoulder.

Sinfully dark, turbulent eyes were fastened on me as Dare's chest rose and fell in quick succession. My skin was awash with electricity at his look—I felt more alive, more aware, than I had in weeks. He seemed to be fighting the urge to pounce on me, and I hoped to god his resolve would shatter. Mine had.

Finding closure could go fuck itself. I wanted Dare.

Right now. And always.

That was not going to change.

eleven

When Dare noticed me looking, he cleared his throat and dropped his gaze. Picking up his palette, he took a sip of coffee then set his cup down. His shoulders stiffened and he shifted in place, as if unsure about his next move. Almost like he wanted to go one way, but knew he should run the other.

"Dare?" I said again, luring him back to me. "Are you okay with this pose?"

He hesitated, opened his mouth, then snapped his jaw shut. Then he took a step toward me, but changed his mind and stayed firmly put.

"Face the wall." The instruction was brief, quiet, and terse.

My chest tightened. He wanted me looking away from him. My smile had been his favorite, but now he couldn't even stand to glimpse it.

Nodding, I pulled a pillow under my head and

closed my eyes, listening to him get to work. The soft hiss of a brush touching the canvas was occasionally punctuated by the scraping sounds of a palette knife. There was a unique music to Dare's work, and as he found his rhythm I could hear him fully relax into it.

And so did I.

God, I remembered this so well. The sounds of him working, the air laced with paint and turpentine. The way his brow would furrow and his lips would tighten as he focused on his work. Time had no meaning or importance in his studio. He'd work for hours without taking a break.

I hoped tonight was no exception.

I'd stay for as long as he'd let me.

I woke to find Dare leaning over me, his hand warm on my hip.

"You fell asleep," he whispered, "and changed your position."

"Oh, shit! I'm sorry." I blinked my hazy vision into focus. "I'm—"

He gave me a gentle nudge. "It's okay." His voice was low, his eyes soft. He was looking at me like he used to, and all I could do was stare back at him, completely entranced by his hypnotic gaze, wildly drawn to his sculpted mouth.

He was so close…if I lifted my head just a little I could touch his lips.

I licked my own just thinking about it.

"Can I…?" he asked, indicating he wanted to guide me back into position. His eyes raked over my body, making me feel even more naked and exposed than I already was.

I couldn't breathe, couldn't speak. So I just nodded.

Yes, you can touch me. Please, please touch me, Dare.

One hand on my shoulder, the other pressed into my back, he directed me up on my side again. The feel of his fingers against my bare skin sent sparks through my body. I inhaled deeply, filling my lungs with him as he moved over me, carefully arranging my body to his liking. His nearness made me dizzy with want, desperate with need. I pressed my thighs together in a feeble attempt to subdue the arousal pulsing between them.

I ached for more of his touch. More of him. *Everywhere.*

When his grip wrapped around my calf, I bit down on my lip to keep from moaning. He shifted my leg so it was resting over the other one, then slid his hand to my knee to lock it in place. He stilled for a moment and turned his head to look at me.

Chocolate-colored eyes pierced me, flooding my

insides with liquid heat. I gasped, unable to hold back the tremor that rocked through me. My whole body was on fire, my most sensitive places throbbing with unbridled desire.

Dare continued to hold my gaze captive, the violent storm in his eyes betraying that he was well aware of his effect on me. A muscle in his jaw twitched, and his grasp on my knee tightened. My pulse kicked up as I imagined him on me, kissing me, parting my legs so he could slip between them...

Oh, god. The tremors flared anew.

But not even a second later, his face turned to stone and he released me. Straightening to his full height, he moved back to his easel, leaving me cold and alone. I was glad my back was to him so he couldn't see my face—couldn't see the disappointment reflected in my eyes.

Dare stayed still for what felt like an eternity. I had to fight every urge to turn and look back at him. Finally, he started painting again, so I shut my eyes and relaxed into the rhythm of his strokes. There was no way in hell I'd be falling asleep again, my mind and body were buzzing with equal parts desire and despair. I lay there thinking about all that had happened three years ago, everything I'd put him through.

I had no idea if I could make up for it, if my

actions could ever be forgiven. Dare had been the one who had come after me even with the threat of my father looming. His life had been at stake, his family had been endangered, yet he'd wanted to fight for me, fight for us.

"I'm sorry," I said, breaking the silence between us.

He was quiet for a moment, then said, "For what?"

For everything.

"For what I said in the hospital."

The painting sounds halted and I heard him inhale sharply.

"Don't, Reagan. Don't go there." His voice was low, dangerous. I'd heard that tone before and knew better than to push him. But how were we supposed to move beyond that if we couldn't even talk about it? If he wouldn't even accept my apology?

I stayed silent and he started painting again.

After a little while he said, "So what happened to make you…like you were in the metro and the other night when the power went out?"

"I…" Cold rigidity settled in my muscles and a lump rose in my throat.

There was one way to make Dare understand just how dangerous and controlling my father really could be—tell him what had happened seven years ago.

But at the mere thought of sharing that part of my past with him—with anyone—my hands began to tremble. I shook my head, begging my heart to calm the fuck down.

I would not think about it. *I would not think about it.* I squeezed my eyes shut to force the images away. Paris. I was in Paris. I was far away from it all. Years and thousands of miles away.

"You don't want to know." My voice came out tight, strained. "Trust me on this."

"I wouldn't ask if I—"

"No, Dare," I said. "Just...*no*. You don't get to shut me down when I apologize, and then pretend like you're concerned about me the next moment. Either you're in or you're out. And you obviously don't want to be in right now." I took a slow, shaky breath. "I deserve that, I know. But you can't have it both ways."

If I told him about what happened, he'd probably forgive me for everything. Right here and now. Maybe he'd even want me back. But I wanted him to want me for *me*—JUST me—not out of pity.

The room turned so eerily still I could hear the soft sounds of traffic from the street below. Night had fallen, and I realized I had no idea what time it was. I heard Dare put down his brushes and palette, so I turned to look at him over my shoulder.

His shoulders were stiff and his eyes unfocused. He seemed...distant. I immediately regretted my angry words. I opened my mouth to say as much, but he beat me to it.

"Why don't we call it a day?" he said. Before I could respond there was a knock on his front door and I could hear it opening.

"Dare?" a husky female voice called out. "*Où êtes-vous?*" *Where are you?*

His head snapped up and he glanced at the doorway to the studio then back to me. Cursing under his breath, he started putting his brushes away as quickly as he could.

"*Ici,* Giselle," he called out. *In here.*

Shit. Giselle? I was about to make a grab for the robe, but she was already standing in the doorway—tall, lithe, and very French. Every hair was perfectly in place, her designer clothes sleek and subdued, she was nothing like...well, me. Her chocolate brown locks were twisted up tight on her head, and her makeup was dramatic and so exact it had to have been put on by an expert. Her green eyes—the only color to her besides the red of her lips—swept over me in distaste.

And I could only imagine what she saw—a naked model with messy hair tumbling around her, looking ridiculously uncomfortable.

Dare finished putting his stuff away, stood up and gave her a quick kiss on the cheek. She grasped his hand and started pulling him out of the room, moaning something about being late.

He glanced at me from the doorway, his face void of expression as he said, "You can let yourself out."

I sat up slowly, watching him. "So...tomorrow?" I said, finally getting hold of the robe and pulling it over me. "Afternoon so I can work in the morning?"

Dare nodded once, and then he was gone.

I heard him say something to Giselle that made her laugh as they walked out the door. I whipped the robe around me and raced to the windows in his living room—the ones that faced the street. As the two of them came out of the building a moment later and walked down the steps, Dare draped his arm over her shoulder and pulled her to him. She slipped an arm around his waist and they walked down the street, disappearing out of sight.

I stood at the window, looking out at the brightly lit street, feeling lonelier than I ever had. That used to be me—the girl in Dare's embrace—but not anymore. I sighed, hugged my arms around myself, and glanced down at the robe.

Ugh. Giselle had probably worn this, too. And suddenly I couldn't stand the feel of it. I hurried toward the bathroom, peeling it away as I went—unable to get it off my skin fast enough.

I dressed and went back to my place to shower. I needed to wash her away.

Giselle. She wasn't his type AT ALL. She was too…artificial. I didn't know how he could stand her. But then again maybe it was her gorgeous body and the way she draped herself over him. Or the way she said his name with that lilt in her voice—like she was caressing it with her French tongue.

Fucking hell. How many times did I have to be hit in the face with how stupid I'd been to let him go?

twelve

"So...have you painted her?" I stood in Dare's studio the next day, my own robe cinched at my waist, the sun's warm rays flooding the futon.

He looked up from his preparations—a new canvas and another pose while we waited for the late afternoon light so we could get back to the painting he'd started yesterday. Dare had a cup of coffee next to him, and I glanced over to find a cup of tea waiting for me again. Its presence warmed me, but then I realized he probably did that for all of his models. It was, after all, just common courtesy. I needed to stop reading into things that weren't actually meaningful.

"Paint who?" he asked, focusing on his brushes again.

"The girl from last night—*Giselle*." It was all I could do to not roll my eyes as I said her name. But I wasn't a sulky teenager...even if I felt like one at the moment.

"I don't paint just anyone," he said quietly, then glanced at me for a brief second before uncovering his palette and nodding toward the futon. "Let's get started."

Not quite sure of what to do with that information, I walked over to the futon feeling utterly off-balance, untied the robe, and let it fall to the ground. Was Dare telling me something? I wanted nothing more than to believe that she didn't mean anything to him, and that *I* did...but...I had nothing to confirm that. He'd left me and spent the evening—and probably the night—with her.

But he didn't paint her? He didn't paint *just anyone?*

What the fuck did that mean?

"Why don't you choose a seated position this time?"

I sat down on the mattress, giving him my profile. One leg crossed over the other and my knee up near my chest where I could rest my chin on it. Staring toward the windows, I closed my eyes and soaked in the sunshine.

Dare was quiet, hadn't started working yet and I couldn't help but wonder if he didn't like the pose. Then I realized that my hair was down, the long honey locks silky against my naked skin and probably blocking too much of my body—the thing about nudes was that you were actually supposed to see the naked form. I reached for my hair to twist it up on my head, but he stopped me.

"Leave it." His command floated across the room, forcing me to turn to look at him. The expression on his face nearly flattened me. It was…it was the exact look he'd captured in those first nudes of his I'd seen in his Brooklyn loft. The one of Sia and the others. *Look at the way they're gazing,* Sabine had said. *It's clearly unrequited love. Sad and bittersweet.*

Dare was wearing that very same expression. It blazed a trail of heat to the depth of my soul. I knew without a doubt that my own look mirrored his. But then his face changed. Hardened. Closed down. And he was, once again, the distant, new Dare I was coming to know.

"Leave the hair," he said again. "I like it down. Wild and free."

I lowered my arms and turned back toward the window, my heart beating too fast for its own good. I took a deep breath, trying to get it to calm the fuck down.

Once Dare began working, I rested my elbow on my knee and leaned my head against my hand to watch him paint. It was a surreal feeling because I could tell he didn't see *me* when he was working. He saw lines, shapes, shadows, light, tones of colors, but not the whole person before him, and I could forget that I was sitting there completely naked. His sharp features softened when he painted, there were no walls, no barriers between us. It was the perfect time to study him.

He glanced up at my face and caught me staring.

And then he smiled just like he used to...and the power of it took my breath away.

That was the look I'd known so well, the one I'd craved ever since I saw him at Montmartre. Warmth flooded my body, bringing with it something I hadn't felt in a long time. I quickly realized that *something* was happiness.

Pure bliss.

But when I started to smile back, the look on his face changed, like he'd caught himself, remembered who I was, what I'd done, and his guard came back up. In a single moment, he filled my heart with hope, and in the next, he knocked the breath out of my lungs.

Why did this have to be so fucking hard? How many times and in how many ways would I have to pay for my sins?

There were so many whys and hows when it came to us. Too many. So I just pushed them all out of my mind and studied him. Took him all in.

Tried to memorize him.

After all, I didn't know how much longer I had with him. Once this project wrapped, we'd go back to existing on our two different planes.

C'est la fucking *vie*, right?

"Dinner?" Dare said, a few hours later as I got up to stretch. Holding a position was not as easy as it looked. I glanced at the clock and was surprised that it was already seven-thirty. I was starving. And I hadn't even noticed. Around Dare, food seemed of little importance.

"Sure." I nodded and he left the studio, walked down the hall and into the kitchen. I could hear him getting out pots and placing them on the stove.

I pulled on my robe and gazed around the room for a moment. Although we'd been working together, I hadn't had much time to look at his newer pieces other than from afar. So I slowly walked around his studio, flipping through the canvases that leaned against the walls. So many street scenes, as I'd noticed in the artists' market, and a handful of nudes.

The models were exquisite, and it sent a jagged, knife-like pain through my soul to think of him sitting in this room with these naked beauties ripe for his picking. God, they even looked turned on, their faces so full of desire as they gazed at me that I could practically hear them moan.

Oh yeah, he'd fucked them. The evidence was right here in front of me, captured in paint.

Pots clanged in the kitchen, turning my attention away, and a large, dark brown fabric-covered sketchbook lying on top of a wooden cabinet caught my eye.

When I lifted the heavy cover to open it, I couldn't believe what I saw inside.

Page after page of sketches…of *me*.

I read over the dates down in the bottom right corner of each drawing. They ranged from a year ago to—*oh, god*—a month ago. Before I'd run into him on the street.

I looked over toward the doorway, heard him opening cabinets in the kitchen.

There were two more identical sketchbooks underneath it, and I flipped each one open to find more sketches of me. From two and three years ago.

Oh. My. God.

Dare had been thinking about me all this time. A LOT. Just like I'd been thinking about him.

I glanced at the nudes on the floor. What if he'd been trying to fuck me out of his head with those models, as I'd been trying to do with random guys for the past three years? From the looks of the latest sketches, he hadn't been able to.

Neither had I.

My heart pounded at that thought. Maybe all wasn't lost. Perhaps I still had a chance.

When I walked into the kitchen, Dare was standing by the stove barefoot, his paint-splattered jeans hanging low off his hips. It was almost painful how amazing he looked, how desperately I wanted to just slip into his arms and slide back into his life. Knowing that he'd been thinking about me so much made the desire that much stronger and made it that much harder to stand there and not touch him.

Get a grip. Focus on getting through dinner. One thing at the time.

Dare had set several different cheeses on the counter next to a carton of milk and a couple of eggs. After he'd placed some fresh parsley and a knife on the cutting board, I realized exactly what he was making.

Macaroni and cheese.

Holy shit.

I stood there in stunned silence. This was a purposeful move, no doubt, but he was so hot and cold with me that I didn't want to get my hopes up.

He noticed me then, and paused in his

preparations, a hunger in his eyes that had nothing to do with food. I couldn't breathe for the hope that filled my entire body in that moment.

"Can I…help?" I asked, and held my breath. Literally.

He stared a few beats more, then nodded toward the cheese. "You want to grate?"

"I'll do anything," I said, and his eyes flicked back to mine. I nodded, wanting him to know I wasn't just talking about dinner.

He made room for me at the counter, and I started grating as he melted butter and mixed in some flour.

I picked up the second cheese. "These are different than what you used to use."

"France has some pretty kickass cheese, so I've been experimenting," he said, pouring milk into the pot. "Wait until you taste this. You'll love it."

Even more hope expanded in my chest, but I didn't know whether to let it fill me or squash it down. Every beat of my heart was fueled by it. My hands shook a little and my breathing became shallow and quick.

I was terrified, I realized. What if I'd read something into this that wasn't really here? What if Dare shot me down again? I wasn't sure I could take it. I needed him like I needed air, like I needed my heart to beat.

He came over next to me and started chopping up the parsley. His arm brushed mine, sending shivers through me. I was suddenly hyper-conscious of the fact that I was practically naked, standing there next to him in the cramped kitchen. A soft layer of silk was the only thing covering me and it was held on by one loose tie. I wondered if Dare had noticed. His arm had stilled next to mine, but he hadn't moved it, like he wanted to touch me as much I wanted to touch him.

I felt simultaneously weak with worry and totally turned on.

"What made you choose Paris?" Dare asked suddenly.

"Art. Sabine." I wasn't sure which had held more sway in the destination I'd chosen. "The fact that I could work for her here helped a lot. It was a way to dip my toes into the business while under the guidance of someone I trusted. Not to mention, it was also far away from…everything."

"So you hadn't heard…" His voice trailed off and at first I didn't know what he was getting at.

"That you were here?" I shook my head. "How would I? You dropped off the radar completely." I focused on grating again, debating whether to say it, and then decided I had nothing to lose at this point. "No, it was just a happy coincidence. If I'd known, I would have come sooner. Much sooner."

Dare inhaled sharply. Fuck. Maybe I shouldn't have said it.

He moved over to the stove and poured the pasta into the boiling water, and I went to sit on a barstool at the counter.

"What about Harvard?" he said as he started making the cheese sauce. "Wasn't that the original plan?"

"That was my dad's dream, not mine."

His lips lifted into a half-smile. "How is the old mayor?"

"Pissed as hell, I'm sure. I haven't spoken with him."

Dare's eyes snapped to mine, his gaze filled with an emotion I couldn't quite identify. "You're really not the same girl, are you." It wasn't a question, and it was said with…god, was it satisfaction?

"I sound stronger than I am." I shrugged. "Honestly, I don't have the guts to talk to him. Or my mother. They'd find ways to pull me back in."

"You're stronger than you think," he said. "Don't ever doubt that."

My cheeks warmed. Though I wasn't sure I believed him, I really liked that he'd said it.

"What about your dad? Is he…out?"

Dare stirred the sauce, didn't respond. He poured the mixture over the pasta and slid the dish into the oven to bake. He set a timer, then came around to sit next to me. A hard lump settled into the pit of my stomach and even though the food smelled amazing, I didn't know if I'd actually be able to eat a single bite. His sharp, angular jaw was tight. He was clearly pissed I'd asked about his dad. Probably because of my dad's threat to release him from prison.

"Dare—"

"My dad's an asshole," he snapped. "I don't want to talk about him."

I shifted to look at him and my robe slipped open a little, exposing my legs. Dare's gaze trailed down my bare skin and he clenched his fists as if fighting with his resolve to not reach out and touch me. My insides heated at his gaze, and my common sense dissolved. I could no longer help myself. I had to push it. Push him.

I uncrossed and re-crossed my legs, the robe slipping further. Dare watched my every move, his Adam's apple bobbing as he swallowed hard. The silence between us was charged. His gaze caressed my legs, slipping up my thighs, scorching me, making my skin tingle everywhere it touched.

I swiveled my body to face him, letting the robe

slip completely open, exposing me from abdomen to ankle. Ever so slowly, I placed my legs on either side of his, totally bared to him as the spot between my legs pulsed with pure need.

I was playing with fire—I knew that—but I was much too drawn to the flame. I had to touch it. Even if that meant getting burned.

Dare's gaze devoured me until something inside him broke free. He reached for me, running his fingers up one thigh, grazing my core, making me gasp, then trailing back down again. He leaned forward, tugged the tie of my robe so the garment slid off my shoulders, exposing me completely. Cupping my breasts in his hands, his thumbs circled my nipples, sending electric currents down to my clit.

Jesus. This was the Dare I knew. The man I remembered.

He pulled me toward him and crashed his mouth to mine, his kiss rough and insistent. I ran my hands over his back, feeling the muscles ripple. I *needed* to touch him. All of him. I grabbed the hem of his shirt and yanked it over his head.

God, he was perfect. I let my hands run over his shoulders and down his sculpted arms, his skin warm and smooth under my touch. Then I trailed them down his chest and over those deliciously hard abs that felt as if they'd been carved out of stone.

With a deep, throaty moan, Dare wrapped both arms around me and crushed me against him. Lowering his head, he licked one breast, blazing a trail with his tongue up and around my nipple. Small whimpers escaped my lips as he possessed it with his warm, wet mouth. He licked and sucked, claiming it as his own, bringing me to the brink of madness as I surrendered to him. My nipples tightened, sending shockwaves of pleasure to my core and I was sure that if he kept doing what he was doing I would come undone at any moment. Just from his freaking mouth.

He moved to my other nipple, teasing it tight with his tongue, nipping the delicate flesh with his teeth. And that most sensitive spot between my legs ached for him with every raspy, gasping breath I drew. I clawed his back, tore my fingers through his hair, needing him closer and closer still.

As if on cue, he stood up and seized my mouth with his. I welcomed him in, opening my lips to taste him. He leaned me back over the counter, his tongue demanding more, delving deeper like he was starved for me. His hand raked through my hair, fisting the locks, pulling me closer, tighter as his other slid between my legs. Two fingers delved deep into my heat as his thumb began to knead my swollen clit.

In this moment, every thought and emotion was filled to the brink with Dare. As he continued to devour every inch of me with unbridled, carnal hunger, I couldn't hold back. I moaned his name. Over and over again.

He groaned when my hands gripped his waistband. One tug and the fly opened, and I sent up a thanks to the gods above for button-fly jeans. They slipped easily past his slim hips, puddling on the floor at his feet.

I bit my lip as I looked down at him.

God. He still went commando. And he was so fucking ready for me.

I took his length in my hands, relishing the feel of the velvet-soft skin of his hardness. He moaned into my mouth, then kissed me harder.

"God, I've missed you so much," I whispered into his lips.

At those words, Dare froze. His body went rigid.

Oh, no.

He took a step back, taking in a shuddering breath and shaking his head.

No, no, no.

"Goddamn it," he said, his face dark with equal parts torture and anger. "I can't fucking go there with you again." He tugged his jeans back up, grabbed his t-shirt, and pulled it on. *"We're* not doing this," he said, waving his hand back and forth between us. "You are my model and that's *all."* He looked at me with a pained, hard glare. "Get the fuck out of my head, Ree."

He stalked out of the room, and a few seconds later I heard the front door slam.

I stood in his kitchen, completely naked, my heart shattering into a million pieces. A cold chill washed over my skin in place of Dare's hands.

He'd called me Ree. That had to mean something.

But, he wanted Ree out. So what did that say about me? About us?

thirteen

The next few days between Dare and me were tense, cold, and business-like. We only saw each other when he needed to paint. If he didn't have the upcoming show, and the impending visit from his siblings, I knew he would have just shown me the door.

But he needed me.

Even if he wouldn't say it. Even if he couldn't admit it. Dare needed me. And I was going to come through for him. This time, I would put his needs ahead of my fears.

I was working for La Période Bleue every day from nine to two, then heading home for a quick shower before going to Dare's where we'd work from three until nine or ten at night. After that, I'd head home to research online for a few more hours. I was not only trying to find artists for Sabine, but I was looking for future talent for my own gallery, and trying to determine where I could afford to start one and whether the communities could support it.

With my limited funds I was looking at a small, humble beginning. If I'd had my father's money behind me, I could have started up in New York or any other big city that had a thriving art community, but that wasn't an option. Even if, by some miracle, he actually came around to approving my chosen career and offered, I still wouldn't accept. My father's money was tainted and always came with strings attached.

This was my dream. I had to achieve it on my own. I needed to know that I could.

Lucien had been getting a little too friendly again, but since I spent most of my time out on the streets, I tried to ignore him. However, every time I was in the gallery, he was right there—talking too close, touching me, asking me to dinner or dancing.

"I'm busy," I kept saying, trying to be polite, stepping out of reach, only to have him step with me. "I'm working every night. I can't."

But he wouldn't take *no* for an answer.

On Wednesday, I stopped by the shop a little after two, before heading home. I'd spent the morning going through a contract with Marie Ormonde, an artist I'd found and totally fallen for. Her paintings were abstracts in bright colors and bold strokes, and gave me that shivery feeling and heart-pounding high I got when I knew with certainty I'd found something great. A hidden talent. I couldn't wait to see her paintings up on the walls at La Période Bleue.

I'd emailed pictures of her work to Sabine and she'd responded with a resounding *Oui!* demanding that I sign Marie on the spot. Looking through the paintings today had me itching to buy some myself, but I couldn't afford to spend the money right now. I made sure to put her contact information in my phone for the future.

I called Sabine from the gallery to check in and let her know how the deal had gone.

"You did well, *chérie!*" she said, and I could hear her beaming at me over the phone. "You are a natural at this, just like I said. I am so proud of you, Reagan. The commission on this show will set you up for your own gallery."

"What do you mean?"

"You are going to get your own commission and the gallery's commission combined. I want you to reap the benefits of your hard work. And I want you to *vivez votre rêve.*" Live your dream. "Say *oui* to it!"

A lump rose in my throat and I couldn't speak for a moment. When I did, my voice was choked. "*Merci beaucoup,* Sabine. Thank you so much. I don't even know what to say."

"Say *oui à l'argent.*" *Yes to the money.*

"*Oui!*" I laughed, even as a couple of tears slipped out. Her belief in me filled me with so much light at that moment that I was certain I could do anything. I would have my own gallery. I would live this life I wanted. I would do it.

We chatted for a few more minutes, catching up, then I said goodbye and hung up the phone. She was the one person in New York that I truly missed. I'd always thought of Archer as my only friend, but I was starting to see maybe that wasn't the whole truth.

A warm, meaty hand grabbed my ass, and I whipped around to find Lucien. Again. Shit. I hadn't even heard him come into the office.

He leaned toward me and I tried to step back but the chair kept me pinned in place. It hit the backs of my knees, knocking me off balance, causing me to fall into the seat. Lucien put his hands on the arm rests and loomed over me.

"*Bonjour, ma belle,*" he said, his stale coffee breath making my stomach churn. "Let us celebrate your first Parisian show tonight. *Que vous et moi.*" *Just you and me.* "I know the perfect way." His gaze slid down my face and neck, and feasted on my chest.

It made my skin crawl.

"I can't," I said, trying to get up out of the chair, but he wouldn't move out of the way.

He leaned even closer. "You must say *oui à* Lucien, too, *chérie.*"

Oh, my god. Had he been eavesdropping on my conversation with Sabine? There was another phone out in the gallery. He must have picked it up and listened in. That was so freaking creepy it chilled me to the bone.

"No," I said, shivers running over my skin. He needed to take a step back and he needed to do it now. "No, I don't. Now get out of my fucking way, Lucien."

His eyes narrowed and he lifted one hand off the armrest as if he were going to grab me, but then the tones rang out in the gallery and a voice called out, "*Bonjour!*"

Lucien shot me a lecherous smile, smoothed back his hair, and walked out of the office to greet the new customer.

When I got to Dare's it was almost five. My hair was still wet, my skin rubbed raw from scrubbing the feel of Lucien off of me.

And I was still shaking.

In the bathroom I'd stared at my bottle of pills. One swallow and I wouldn't feel anything at all, but

Dare would know. He'd see. And he'd be disgusted.

Three years ago, doctors had suggested a treatment center. You didn't need a medical degree to know that the pills were just bandaids for deeper wounds that would not heal. But my mother wouldn't hear of it. What would people think if gossip spread about a McKinley needing help? Her solution was more pills. How fucked up was that?

So instead, I had pulled the phoenix out of my purse and spread it out on the counter in front of me. THIS was true strength—the ability to recreate oneself. I was trying—good god, I was TRYING. But those fucking pills would make everything so much simpler. They called to me, my old friends.

However, Dare was so much more important. I couldn't fuck this up. Without a doubt, I knew I'd never see him again if I walked over there high. My phoenix would just have to do. I folded the paper back up and put it in my pocket. Having it with me would help.

Hopefully.

"You're *late*." Dare didn't bother to look at me, he just growled in my direction when I entered the studio and hurried over to the futon.

"I'm s—"

"Save it," he said. "If you're not going to be

reliable, then I can't use you. I'll have to find someone else or…say fuck it to this show." I stared at him, unspeaking. "Or I'll just have to paint anyone because who gives a shit? A nude is a nude, right? No one fucking cares as long as they get to buy a painting of a naked woman."

"You care." My voice shook just a little and my eyes were stinging. "And I do, too."

"The hell you do. We've lost a lot of light because you're late. We can't work on one of the paintings because of that. If you actually cared you'd be here on time."

The shaking started again, no matter how hard I tried to hold it in, it wouldn't stop. I put my hand in my pocket and held on to the phoenix.

I turned away from him, not sure what to do. Did he not want me here? I didn't want to go back to my apartment by myself, not after today. I couldn't stand to be alone. I wasn't sure I would be able to resist the pills if left on my own.

Because I didn't want to feel this way—I didn't want to feel *anything*.

Dare was quiet for a moment, then I heard the scrape of his stool and footsteps across the floor. I blinked my eyes furiously, willing them to stay dry. I did not want to fall apart, but I couldn't seem to stop it from happening.

"I'm sorry," he said in a quiet voice from

behind me. He didn't reach out to touch me, and for once I was glad—there was no way I'd be able to hold it together if he did. "I'm just…stressed. I shouldn't take it out on you."

I nodded, unable to find my voice as I tried to untie my robe. My shaking hands failed to cooperate as I yanked and pulled at the tie around my waist, suddenly feeling like I couldn't breathe. It was too tight—why had I tied it so fucking tight?—and it needed to come off NOW. My breathing quickened as I fought with both my belt and the tears of frustration that threatened to erupt.

I choked out a sob, and Dare stilled my hands. He reached out from behind me to gently untie the belt and set me free. Air rushed into my lungs and I could breathe again. Dare spun me around, took hold of my hands. He stared at them quaking in his larger ones for a few beats, then looked up at my face.

Seeing my expression, his eyes widened. "Shit. What's wrong? Did I do this?"

I shook my head and swallowed. Taking a deep breath, I found my center. "Not everything is about you, Princess," I said, and he almost smiled.

"What happened?"

I wrapped my arms around my body and shrugged. "Just a really bad day at work."

As I told him about Lucien, Dare's shoulders stiffened and his eyes got dangerously dark—I could feel the anger vibrating through him, rolling off him in intensely vicious waves.

"I'm picking you up from work tomorrow," he said, his jaw tight. "I'll have a talk with the asshole."

"You don't have to do that." I shook my head. "It's fine."

"It's NOT fine. That guy needs to be put in his place."

"I don't want to cause problems," I told him. I had no idea what Dare's intentions with Lucien were, and I couldn't be responsible for Dare getting blacklisted from the Parisian art scene.

"You're not the one causing the problems. He is." He studied my face. "Do you want to take today off? If you're not up for this right now, it's fine."

"Honestly, I'd rather work. And you need to work. I'm okay." I slipped the robe off my shoulders and let it fall to the floor, only belatedly thinking about the fact that I'd be standing naked right next to him when I did.

Dare looked down at my body, his gaze heating. The feel of his eyes on my skin had the power to erase all that had happened, and I forgot about everything but him. I could feel the warmth from his body as if it were caressing my bare skin, peaking my nipples and making me pulse in my most private places.

My voice was breathless when I said, "How do you want me?"

His eyes flicked up to mine, and the hunger I saw there matched my own. He swayed toward me, like he was lulled by my nearness, but then he shook himself, ran his hands through his hair, and took a step back.

"Let's do a new pose tonight. Something comfortable. Something…free." He backed away to his easel, slipped behind it, safe in his world of shapes and shadows, color and light.

I lay down on the futon, on my back, my hair spread out around my head, one arm resting on my abdomen, the other hanging off the edge of the mattress. I watched him work, listening to the rhythm of his strokes, dreaming it was his hands on my body instead of his brushes on canvas.

fourteen

I spent the next morning checking out artists that Marie had recommended to me. One of them, a guy named Jean-Pierre, had serious potential. He worked mostly in watercolors and specialized in landscapes. While I didn't usually find that subject particularly fascinating, his paintings really caught my eye.

I wasn't even sure what it was—a combination of the loose style and palette perhaps. Or maybe it was his use of shadow and light. I couldn't narrow it down to only one thing that spoke to me.

Art, like love, was one of those undefinable things in life. Sometimes it was just about the feeling it gave you, and YOU alone. The kind of feeling that made your heart beat to a different tune, and the entire world look just a tiny bit brighter. His art was like that, and I was pretty certain I'd be setting up a show for him, too.

When I returned to the gallery after lunch, I was giddy with excitement over my new find, feeling like I was in the right place, and that things were finally syncing. I confirmed some details with Marie over the phone, then spent a good hour filling out paperwork for her show.

The gallery was eerily quiet, and I suddenly became aware of him behind me, lurking.

"Lucien, I'm busy right now," I said, my voice tight. "Please leave."

His hands slid onto my shoulders, sending a shudder down my spine. I shrugged him off, and turned to look at him.

And that's when I noticed the office door was closed.

My eyes flew to his, goosebumps prickling over my skin, my heart starting to pound. Something about this felt very wrong. Cold fear flooded my veins as I forced myself to breathe and stay in control.

I tried to keep calm as I said, "I'm working. I've got to get this done."

"Ah, but you work too hard, *chérie*," he said, his voice like oil—slippery smooth and leaving a slimy residue. "I can help you relax." He stepped closer.

"No." I quickly stood, placing my chair between us. "I don't need to relax." I glanced at the clock on the desk. Shit. It was already two-thirty. Dare would be here any minute. "I need to finish this so I can go home."

"What are you doing every night that you do not have time for your good friend Lucien?"

"I'm modeling for an artist," I said, slowly inching toward the door.

Lucien's eyes lit up, and he raked his gaze down the length of me, undressing me with unabashed boldness.

He stepped toward me again. "How about you model for me sometime, *chérie?*"

"You're not an artist." You're just a perv.

"But of course I am," he said, reaching out to touch me, "and you would be my perfect muse. Nude, yes?"

I darted for the door, but he got there first, his hands grabbing my arms, pulling me against his body. Oh, god. Revulsion shook me as I felt his erection against my stomach and I pushed against him as hard as I could.

"Let go of me!" I screamed, panic filling my chest. The tighter he held me, the more I struggled. I stomped on his foot and he cursed, releasing me just as the tones rang out in the gallery.

I yanked the door open as Lucien's hand cracked across my cheek sending me crashing into the doorframe, tumbling out onto the gallery floor. Stars sparked behind my eyes as the shock of the blow stunned me. The sound of fists meeting flesh and Lucien moaning on the floor brought me back.

Someone was hovering over me.

"Are you okay?" Dare's brow was crinkled in concern, his eyes flashing. "What did he do to you? Do I need to call the police?"

I shook my head. "I'm okay. He just…" I started shaking then, thinking about what Lucien had been about to do, what he might have done if Dare hadn't come in just then. My breathing went from zero to full-out hyperventilation in about 2.6 seconds. Darkness threatened at the edges of my vision as pins and needles spread through my fingers and toes.

Dare wrapped his arms around me and held on tight. "Put your head down," he said. "Breathe into your hands—I don't have a bag." He rubbed my back, and I could feel his calm seeping into my body from his warm hands. "You're safe, Ree. I've got you."

By the time we got back to our apartments, I could breathe again.

It was over. I was fine.

I'd called Sabine and she'd fired Lucien on the

spot, ensuring me she would make certain he could never work in another gallery again. I don't know what Dare had said or done to him behind the closed office door while I was on the phone with Sabine, but Lucien left in a hurry without even looking at me. It was such a relief to know I wouldn't have to deal with him anymore.

I went to my place to take a shower, then headed over to Dare's apartment. He glanced up in surprise when I entered his studio. The moment his gaze fell on my face, worry flashed in his eyes. A bruise had formed on my cheek where Lucien had hit me. Dare got up to get a closer look, gently prodding it with his fingers. All I wanted to do was close my eyes and sink my heated cheek into his palm, but I held back.

I had no idea where we stood. He'd saved me today and I couldn't contain the immense gratitude I felt. It didn't fit neatly into a box, a *thank you*, or an embrace. It overflowed and filled the studio, seeping into everything I saw and touched.

It colored my world.

"Do you want some ice for that?" he asked. Then he looked down at my robe. "What are you doing? We're not working tonight. I want you to take a break. It's—"

"I want to, Dare." I owed him so much—

everything. Not only had he helped me today, but he was the reason I wasn't reaching for my pills right now. Most importantly, he had been the inspiration for my break for freedom from my family. I never would have followed the art if I hadn't met him. He'd saved my life in more ways than one.

I wanted to do better, be better, because of him.

So, yeah. I wanted to be here.

"Go get set up," I said as I walked over to the futon to take off my robe. Dare stayed glued to the floor, looking unconvinced. "Dare," I said. "There is no other place I'd be rather be right now. Please."

He hesitated a moment more, then walked back over to his easel as I got settled on the futon. I lay on my back again and watched him, wondering how I could ever repay all that he'd given me. This—being here for him to paint—was the least I could do. And I hadn't been kidding when I'd said this was where I wanted to be.

I only wanted to be here.

With Dare.

The wine cellar. Complete darkness. I'm shivering from the cold. So, so dark. Why does it have to be so dark in here? Why did he turn off the lights when he came in?

He whispers and I jump. I can't see him. But I feel him.

Hands. There are hands everywhere. I can't stop them from touching me, from ripping at me and tearing me apart.

I try to scream, but there's a heavy weight on my chest.

No. No, no, no…

Please no!

Can't breathe, can't yell for help. Can't—

I woke with a jolt, sat up gulping in air like I'd been holding my breath. Shit. Was he still here? I couldn't feel his hands anymore, but that didn't mean he was gone.

Someone stirred next to me and I scrambled out of bed, falling to the floor with a *thud.*

Dare sat straight up, looked down at me and jumped out of bed.

Dare?

Oh, god. I thought—it had seemed like—*damn it*, I was all mixed up. It had been a dream. Just a fucking dream. Thank god for that.

The room was dark, curtains drawn, but I could see light filtering in around them from the streetlamps.

Where was I?

Wait, if Dare was here then…I was in Dare's bed.

Holy fucking shit. How did I end up in Dare's bed?

"What's wrong?" he asked as he knelt down beside me. "Nightmare?"

I looked at him, the remains of the dream fading away. "What am I doing here?"

"You fell asleep while we were working," he said. "It was really late, so I carried you in here." He shrugged. "I didn't think you wanted to be alone."

"I don't." I slowly got to my feet and he stood with me. My throat felt thick with emotion. "Thank you. Again."

We stood there staring at each other, the intensity reaching an all-time high. I felt this incredible pull toward him—a kind of magnetic attraction. And it seemed as if he did, too.

But I could still feel his hesitation, and I didn't know what to do about it. In all honesty, I was exhausted from trying to figure it out.

"It's—" He looked like he was searching for the right words but wasn't sure what they were. "It was the right thing to do." Then he smiled. "I know how you are about that."

Oh, my god. Was he actually teasing me?

"Yeah, whatever." I rolled my eyes, feeling the warmth of his grin seep through my body right down to my bones. "All I did was lend you my freaking car. You *needed* it, Dare. Admit it. I can't believe you're still going on about that three years later."

His eyes widened as he let out a small laugh, suddenly looking a lot more like the Dare I knew so well. It felt so good to joke with him. Everything that had happened today disappeared from my mind. There was only Dare.

"It was a cherry red Mercedes SLS AMG," he said. "A three-hundred-thousand-dollar car. There weren't any of those in my neighborhood."

I shrugged my shoulders and pointed to my chest. "Well, *this* court saw fit to award it to you in rightful exchange while your car was being fixed, thanks to the fucked up driving of the defendant."

Dare laughed. "I still object on the grounds that the gesture was way too extravagant."

"Overruled. The grace period for filing complaints has passed." I banged an invisible gavel in the air. "You're just going to have to let it go."

He arched an eyebrow. "Jesus. You sure you're not going to law school?"

I nodded. "More sure than ever. You've just forgotten how good I am at arguing."

"Your stubbornness is impossible to forget, Ree." He smiled at me then, the warm, wonderful smile of three years ago when everything was good.

I held my breath, waiting for his face to close again, for him to shut down on me, to remember why he didn't want to be with me anymore. He didn't. Instead, he just climbed back into bed, held the covers up for me as an invitation, and waited.

The scariest thing I'd ever done was walk back over and slip in beside him, not knowing whether it would be this old, warm Dare or the new, closed-off Dare I'd wake up to in the morning. But something felt different, things had changed between us, so I took a chance.

He pulled me tight against him, his hands staying still, showing no intent to take things further that night. I relaxed into his embrace, and fell asleep again, listening to the rhythm of his breaths, relishing the feel of his warmth around me.

Existing in this moment with Dare was like coming home after a long journey, like being lost and suddenly found again.

fifteen

The next afternoon the butterflies were back in my stomach as I was getting ready to go over to Dare's. Things felt so different. GOOD different. We'd woken up late, and I'd had to rush to get to the gallery, but he'd still looked at me like he wanted me there. Like he was sorry to see me go.

The new Dare was gone. The old one was back, mostly, and I couldn't wait to spend the evening with him. My body was humming, already tingling in all the right places as I envisioned all the things I wanted to do to him—and have him do to me—after he was done painting.

Things just felt right, like tonight would lead us forward. Together. And I couldn't wait to get started on that journey.

As my hand reached for the doorknob, there was a knock on my door. Excitement flooded me as I grinned. Dare couldn't wait either. Maybe we wouldn't make it to the painting at all tonight.

Maybe we'd spend the entire afternoon doing all the naughty things I'd—

"Reagan! Open up, baby girl! I've come to rescue you."

My jaw dropped and my mouth literally hung agape as I opened the door to Archer.

"What are you—"

"Get dressed, babe. I'm taking you out." He breezed past me to stand in the middle of my living room. As always, every minute detail about him—from his expensive clothes to his precisely arranged blonde waves—was executed to perfection. He was like a living, breathing magazine shot. Even his wrinkled up nose as he evaluated my apartment was somehow attractive. "I've flown all the way to Paris just for this."

I stood frozen in the open doorway. "How the hell did you—"

"Know where you were? I'm a resourceful guy." He looked past me as I heard Dare's door open. "This place is a dump. Why don't you come stay with me at the George V? I've got a huge suite and I'm willing to share my bed." His lascivious grin was aimed over my shoulder.

I turned to see Dare standing in his doorway, his face stony, his eyes full of betrayal. I opened my mouth to explain that this obviously wasn't what it looked like, but his gaze turned cold, and he just shook his head like he couldn't believe he'd fallen for it again.

"Dare," I said, taking a step toward him, "wait…it's not—"

"It's not what, Reagan? Jesus Christ, what do you take me for?"

I rushed across the hallway to his door, and spoke in a low voice. "It's not what you think. He just showed up. He's my fr—"

"I *know* who he is. I remember him very clearly."

OH, SHIT. The last time Dare had seen Archer had been at the hospital after my overdose. When Archer had claimed me as "his girl." Which meant Dare probably thought we'd been together this whole time. And that I was still with him since he was practically marking my apartment as his territory. It REALLY didn't help that Dare had caught the tail end of our conversation and heard Archer's flippant proposition.

Things hadn't even gotten started for real with Dare and life was already screwing with me. Fucking hell.

"I didn't know he was coming to Paris, Dare. And I definitely didn't know he'd just show up at my apartment unannounced." I glanced back at Archer and he winked.

Fuck. Me.

"Jacques just called," Dare said, ignoring my explanation. "I have to head over to the gallery for a couple of hours. I won't need to you model right now, so you and Pretty Boy can do whatever the hell you want."

I sighed. "Do you still want to work on the paintings later tonight? I'll just grab a quick dinner with Archer and meet you when you get back."

Dare's eyes bore into mine. "Do what you want." He stepped past me to close and lock his door. Then he stuffed his apartment keys in the pocket of his jeans and stalked away, disappearing down the stairwell.

SHIT.

Taking a deep breath, I plastered a smile I wasn't truly feeling on my face, and turned back to Archer. "So," I said, dreading the night and already wishing it was over.

He searched my face as if he saw through my grin. "Everything okay, baby girl?"

My foul mood wasn't fair to Archer. Meeting my old—and only—friend for dinner wasn't unreasonable. Dare would just have to understand or keep his brooding to himself. While I didn't exactly want to be rocking the boat at *this moment* in our re-relationship, this dinner was the right thing to do. In order to have a real shot with Dare, I had to be able to fully exist and function apart from him.

"Yes. Everything is fine," I told Archer with a real smile this time. "Where do you want to go for dinner?"

"I've already made reservations at Le Cinq, so slip into something sexy and let's go." He looked me up and down, then lifted a mischievous eyebrow. "You need some help getting changed?"

"Hell no," I said, pushing him toward the couch, and laughed in spite of everything. God, he was such a fucking rogue. I was worried about Dare and how I'd smooth things over later, but Archer could always make me laugh. Even in the worst of times. I hadn't realized just how much I'd missed him.

I went into my room and put on my favorite vintage, champagne-colored silk sheath dress. It fit like a glove, the color a perfect complement to the golden tones of my long, straight hair. I hadn't been anywhere as nice as Le Cinq since I'd left New York—and it felt kind of good to dress up.

Though all I could think was, *I wish Dare was coming.* I wanted him to be the one admiring me from across the table, not Archer.

But I couldn't think like that. I'd see him later, and I wanted to enjoy dinner. Even if it had to be mostly by force of will.

Archer kept up a funny and distracting dialogue all through dinner. However contrived, it felt good to laugh with him. He had a PhD in Charm and even though I could always see through his bullshit, I understood why women fawned over him. In fact, I noticed several cougars near our table who kept trying to catch his eye—one of whom looked older than his mother, which only made me tease him until he blushed.

"Oh my god," I said, staring in amazement at his flushing cheeks. "You've actually fucked somebody's mom, haven't you? God, just please don't tell me it was mine." My curiosity got the better of me as I leaned toward him and whispered, "So how was it?"

"Fan-*fucking*-tastic," he said, laughing. "But nothing compared to you. You know you're the only girl for me."

"Not true, as evidenced by the long line of chicks who came before and after me," I said. "But someday, some girl will steal your heart and that statement will be so very true for her."

Archer stared at me for a moment, before looking down at his empty plate. "Dessert?"

"No way." I shook my head. "*J'ai fini*. That meal was so amazing I don't have any room for dessert.

But you go ahead if you want."

He tilted his head and cocked an eyebrow. "There's only one thing I want for dessert and it's not on the menu."

I groaned so loudly a few people actually turned to look at us. "Does that line ever work?"

He grinned, his blue eyes glinting. "Every single time, baby girl. Don't bust my perfect record now. Come on, be a team player."

"God. Grow up." Being the adult I was, I threw my napkin at him. "You're depraved, you know that?"

"And you love that about me."

I rolled my eyes. "You wish."

"I do, actually." The gravity in his tone made the smile fall from my face.

Not this, Archer. Not now.

He shrugged and signaled to our waiter for the bill as my phone rang.

Fucking A—Mother aka *Don't Pick Up if You Know What's Good For You* as she was now labeled in my contacts. I'd been ignoring her phone calls since the day I left New York. So far, I'd collected twenty-one livid voicemails. Every single one was delivered in that terrifyingly quiet, icy tone she loved to use on me.

"You better have a good excuse for this impromptu trip, Reagan."

"Your father wants to know why you have failed to respond to Harvard, Reagan."

"Why can't you be more like your siblings, Reagan? Quincy and Pierce would NEVER do this to me. I am having daily migraines because of your selfish behavior."

The last few were just: "Reagan. Call me. NOW."

Two days ago, my mailbox had finally reached its Olivia McKinley limit.

I turned the screen around to show Archer and he nodded at it.

"You should probably just talk to her and get it over with," he said. "You're going to have to eventually."

I narrowed my eyes at him. How the hell did he know I hadn't been talking to her all along? I looked down at my vibrating phone again. Oh, what the fuck.

"Hello, Mother."

"Reagan. Finally!" There was something eerily different about the pitch of her voice this time. It had none of the frost of her voicemails. "How are you, darling?"

Darling? My mother had never once in my twenty-two years called me *darling.* Or anything else that could be deemed a term of endearment. A warning flashed in my mind. Something was up. Something HAD to be up.

"Fine," I said.

"And how are things with Archer?"

"He just got here today. How did you know he was here?" My stomach clenched as I realized *exactly* how she knew. My gaze pinned Archer in place.

"I heard you were having a lovely dinner at Le Cinq."

"Heard?" I glared across the table. *Traitor.*

"Yes. *Très romantique!* Soooo," she said, drawing out the word as if it had eleven fucking o's, "do you have any news?"

"News?" I paused, raising my eyebrows at Archer. The smile froze on his face and he quickly busied himself with the bill. And I turned my attention back to her. "Mother, have you taken too many of your special pills?"

And then she laughed—this tinkling, high-pitched giggle she only used when she was kissing up to donors and politicians. If this wasn't a sign that she'd lost her freaking mind...

"Oh, Reagan! I miss your sparkling sense of humor."

Yeah, right. She hated my sense of humor with a passion. Had often referred to my sarcasm as "sickeningly inappropriate."

I clenched my fingers around the phone. "Is

there something you need?"

"Why would you think that?" My mother had a gift for sounding wounded. "I was simply calling to see how you were doing—as I have been *for weeks*—and ask if you had anything to tell me."

"What exactly do you want to hear about? How my gallery work is going? It's great, actually. Thanks for asking."

"Oh, Reagan. You cannot still be serious about that, can you? You know, you can still go to Harvard in the fall. Your father contacted them right away to hold your spot."

"*What?!* I told them I wasn't coming."

"I know. And that was awfully rash of you. We should all get together—you, Archer, your father, and I—to talk about it. Your future is too important."

What the fuck did Archer have to do with my future?

She wasn't making any sense. "Mother, what do you REALLY want?"

"Look at the time! I have got to run. Your father and I are hosting a dinner tonight and I must get to my stylist. *Au revoir.*" She hung up before I could say anything else.

I stared at my phone for a moment, my mouth hanging open as I tried to make sense of the bizarre call. My mother was mixing meds, no doubt about it.

"Everything okay?" Archer asked.

I frowned at him. "My mother didn't ask about Paris or try to talk me into coming home. Instead, she wanted to talk about you and the dinner reservations you made. Why is that, Arch?"

His eyes widened for just a moment, but then he simply shrugged. "Sounds like someone took too many happy pills."

"You've been talking to her behind my back. She sent you here, didn't she." It wasn't a question—I already knew the answer.

"Just to ensure you're all right," he said as he reached for my hands. I pulled them off the table and placed them in my lap. "Your parents have been worried, Reagan."

I scoffed. "Not about me! They're worried for themselves. And how my little escape from the McKinley clutches could mess with *their* plans."

"Yeah, but—"

"Forget it." I shook my head. "I'm in Paris. I officially don't want to think about my mother anymore. Just don't be her spy, okay? Don't do that to me. You're my friend, don't be my Benedict fucking Arnold. I don't care if I suddenly find myself in the middle of a freaking *Taken* plot. Don't talk to my parents about me. That's not a request."

"Okay, I won't. Scout's Honor." He saluted me and laughed, but when he stood up and came over to pull my chair out, he looked…off.

I glanced up at him. "You all right?"

His mask slipped back into place and he aimed a dazzling smile at me. "Perfect as always."

I was about to retort that *perfect* was not the word I'd choose to describe this moment, but something in his expression stopped me. So I said nothing.

As we walked out to the lobby of the hotel, he tried to talk me into going up to his suite, but I begged off.

Dinner was over, I'd fulfilled my friendly obligation, and I could feel Dare waiting for me on the other side of the Seine.

Hopefully.

sixteen

The streets of Paris sparkled with lights, but I took no notice as I hurried back to Dare's apartment, my heart hammering more from nervousness than exertion. I didn't even bother going back to my place first to change; I just knocked on his door as soon as I reached the top of the steps.

The door flew open and Dare stood before me, shirtless, towel in hand, his jeans hanging low. I drank him in, tan skin stretched over the muscular terrain of his torso, all jagged mountains and smooth valleys. He was so fucking beautiful. Archer may have been picture perfect, but Dare was living and breathing art. Sensual. Powerful. Erotic.

He glared at me for a moment, his eyes narrowed as he took in my wild hair and slinky dress. Then he opened the door wider to let me in, and I stepped past him. When he shut it, I turned to tell him how sorry I was about this evening, but he was suddenly right there, inches away, rendering me speechless.

We stared at each other in silence for a moment, the air between us so charged it was practically crackling. The pull of Dare was so strong it was a wonder I was able to stand on my own.

"Are you and he...?" His eyes were dark, fathomless.

"NO," I said, shaking my head. "*No.*"

"Because it seemed like—"

"It's not."

His gaze slid to my lips and I held my breath.

"He's from *your* world," he said.

"It's not my world anymore. I'm out. TOTALLY out."

"It didn't look like it."

"I am. I sw—"

Before I even finished speaking he descended on me, his hands grasping my face, his mouth crashing into mine as he pushed me back, pressing me hard against the door.

His hands slid down the sides of my body until he reached the hem of my dress and tugged the slippery fabric up over my hips. Then he grabbed the waist of my lace thong in both hands, tearing it completely off of me.

I had never been more turned on by the sound of ripping fabric.

He threw the ruined panties behind him as I wrapped my legs around his waist. He cupped my bare ass in his hands, lifting me higher, pushing me harder against the door, opening me wider. I rubbed myself against him, begging for him to take me.

Roughly pulling my dress over my head, Dare broke our kiss only to free the fabric and toss it aside. His hands sought my breasts, his fingers teasing my nipples to hard, tingling buds. I raked my nails over his back, digging into his hard muscles as he took one nipple into his mouth and sucked on it until I was a moaning, writhing puddle of pure desire.

He kissed me again, hooking his hands behind my knees and carried me, naked and wrapped around him, to the couch. As he laid me down on the cushions, covering my body with his much larger one, he blazed a trail of kisses up my jawline and down my neck to my chest.

One hand wove into my hair while his other slid down to my thigh, pulling it up and to the side, completely exposing me to him. Liquid heat blazed in his eyes, and he let out a low moan as his fingers delved between my folds. His thumb massaged my clit, two fingers caressing my opening with expert strokes.

"Jesus, Ree." His hot, minty breath caressed my neck. "You're so fucking wet." I bucked my hips, urging him inside, whimpering for him to have his way with me. "And so very impatient." His lips curved into a satisfied smirk as he drove his fingers into me, quenching my thirst for him while setting fire to my entire body with quick, deep thrusts.

All for you, I wanted to say, but my words were reduced to moans as he increased the speed and intensity of his touch. As he unraveled me from the inside, he bit down on my bottom lip, sucking it to the same rhythm of his fingers.

I wrapped my arms around his neck and crashed his mouth to mine in a bruising kiss, melding us together. No matter how much he gave me, it wasn't enough. I wanted more of him, needed him closer.

Just when I thought I had him, he stilled his fingers inside me and pulled back. "What do you want?" His voice seductively low and husky, his dark eyes piercing my soul.

"You," I said. "You, Dare."

"Good answer." He rewarded me with a storm of kisses down my stomach and paused right above the one place I wanted his mouth the most right now. It throbbed in rhythm with my hammering heart, aching for him to lick it, suck it. I lifted my hips. Offering. Begging.

"Please," I whispered.

"Tell me what you want me to do to you." His words were rough, demanding.

"Lick me."

A wicked grin filled his face as he lowered his head and ran his tongue along my folds, swirling it around my swollen clit, pressing his smile into me. My body detonated, little explosions going off everywhere as my core tightened in anticipation. Dare licked me again, his warm tongue flicking lightly across my clit.

"I want to hear you say you want me again. Louder this time."

"I want you." I moaned as he licked me again.

"Tell me you want *only* me." His teeth grazed me, nipping at the sensitive flesh.

"I do." Oh, god. His fucking *mouth*. "I want you, Dare. Only you. Always you."

His warm breath on my ache drove me wild. Moaning, I lifted my hips and sought out his mouth, sighing with relief and elation when he licked me again.

"What else do you want, Ree?" His voice was deep and carnal, dripping with sex. The sound alone made me throb harder, pulse faster, writhe more.

"Suck," I said. "Please."

He grinned and lowered his head, parted my thighs even wider, then took my clit between his lips and ever so gently sucked. Stars exploded behind my eyes. The more he sucked, nibbled, and licked, the stronger the current flowing through me grew. My hips rocked against his mouth to the rhythm he set. My moans rose higher and higher, until I was certain the entire freaking building could hear me.

Fuck if I cared.

My whole world was Dare—there was nothing else in this moment or the next but him. Just him. He'd been the only person in my life who could make me feel this way, who could make me forget everything else.

"Say my name, Ree," he said, his voice strumming my insides. "I want you to scream it when you come."

He licked me again—hard and fast—and I was suddenly coming undone. I cried out his name over and over again as the tingling inside me built to a fevered pitch, exploding in an intense wave that crashed through my body and made me lose feeling in my fingers and toes.

Dare watched me carefully as the wave subsided, his eyes hooded, a soft, satisfied smile sprawled across his face.

And, in that moment, I knew.

He was mine.

I was his.

We were back.

I reached for his jeans and freed him. He stood before me magnificently naked, all solid muscle and unadulterated arousal. I nearly cried out when he walked away and out of the room, but he was back in seconds, a condom in his hand.

I seized it from him, more than ready to finally have him inside me. But before I put it on, I first took him in my hands, kissed him with my lips. He moaned as I ran my hands up and down his length, indulging in a taste of him. He was rock-hard, so ready for me. So perfect. I loved that I did this to him.

"Ree," he said, and I thrilled at my name on his lips, at his worshipping plea.

I ripped open the package, pulled the condom out, and smoothed it over his erection. He leaned me back, claiming my lips again with his own as he placed himself between my legs.

I could feel him at my opening, pressing lightly—just enough to make me crazy with want—and I reached down to guide him in. He filled me completely, causing me to cry out in pleasure as he pushed all the way in.

God. He felt so fucking good.

Dare kissed me hard, possessing me with his whole body, with the rhythm of his movements, and I met him kiss for kiss, thrust for thrust. In this moment, it was as if we had the power to erase years of cold, empty distance. Our combined passion took us higher and higher until he was moaning my name and I was crying out his as we rocked together in exquisite release.

He collapsed on me, our skin slightly sweaty, our bodies depleted, our breathing slowing in sync. I wrapped my arms and legs around him, refusing to let go, trying to hold myself together as much as hold onto him.

But when he gently nuzzled into my shoulder, kissing my collar bone just like he used to—a little thing that no one else had ever done, that felt so sweet, so intimate, so…caring—I lost it. Tears spilled down my face, dripping into his hair, and my body was racked with silent sobs. I'd missed him so much. The past three years had felt as if I was missing half of my heart, half of my soul. Having him back in my life was overwhelming in the best possible way.

"Shh," he said as he held me in a soothing, tight embrace. "It's okay, Ree. I'm here."

And that just made me cry harder. He *was* there. We were finally together and I finally felt like my life was falling into place.

seventeen

Even before my eyes opened the next morning, I could hear the soft scratch of pencil on paper, the smudge of fingers softening shadows and lines. And I knew—he'd been drawing me as I slept. Happiness flooded me, filling in all the spaces from the top of my head to the tips of my toes. The black hole was gone—in its place was an incredible feeling of wholeness.

I was smiling when I finally looked at him.

My real smile. The one that only Dare brought out in me.

When he glanced up and saw me watching him, he put down his pad, and came back over to the bed. He wore nothing but shorts, and I watched the way his muscles rippled as he crossed the room. I was reaching for him before he got to me, anxious to touch him, needing to feel him, to make certain that he was real.

That we were real. That this was really happening.

My god. It *was* really happening.

"Good morning." He leaned down kiss my lips.

I laughed and turned my head to the side. "I haven't even brushed my teeth yet," I said as he nuzzled my neck, sending shivers over my skin. I tried to roll away, but he trapped me, bringing his face right down to mine.

"I don't care, Ree," he said, the most beautiful smile lighting his face. "I'm fucking starved for you. I want you just the way you are."

"Dirty?"

"And naked." His eyes darkened. "Very, very naked."

"And free," I said, for the first time in my life feeling truly *free*.

I stared up at him, my gaze settling on his lips. When he slowly leaned down to kiss me, it was like he was drinking me in, exploring me for the first time. I opened my mouth to welcome him in, feeling my body awaken in all the right places.

And as he slid into the bed beside me, his hands exploring my contours, I finally felt like everything—EVERYTHING—was right in my world.

"So, will you have enough?" I was facing him this time, sitting with my arms crossed over my legs, my long hair tumbling down all around me, sunlight raining down, highlighting the right side of my body.

"Paintings?" Dare said, focusing on the canvas. "Yes. I talked to Jacques this morning and the show is a go." He looked relieved. "I've just got to finish this one, and refine a couple of the others. Should be able to do that over the next few days."

I grinned. I couldn't help it—I was so excited about his show. It was a huge deal even if Dare wasn't acting like it. I knew better.

"So then what's next for Dare Wilde?" I asked softly.

He shrugged, squinted at his work for a moment, then spoke. "I guess I'll have to see what happens. Rex wants me to visit some friends of his while I'm in Europe. So, I'm not sure." He was cautious, not making any plans, not committing.

Not sure of me still.

Not sure of us.

Intellectually, I understood, but that didn't mean my heart was protected from the hurt.

Because *I* was sure of us. After everything we'd been through, after three years apart, after finding each other again in Paris, of all places...I was sure.

I wanted Dare.

Without question. Without doubts. Without end.

But would he come to feel the same?

Dare's phone rang. He glanced down at the screen and his face lit up.

"You want to stretch?" He put down his brushes and reached for the phone. "This'll just be a minute." Then he tapped the screen. "Dash!" he said, and turned toward the windows. "How's life as a rock god?"

I pulled my robe around me, grabbed Dare's mug, and went to the kitchen to refill his coffee and get more tea. I loved being in his space, feeling like I belonged. Almost. Clearly he wasn't as all-in as I was, and that was okay. I'd hurt him last time—he had every right to tread cautiously.

But standing in his kitchen, feeling at home here…it filled me in a way nothing else ever had.

When I came back to the studio he was still on the phone.

"Amsterdam? I don't know, man. I've got…" He looked at me. "…*stuff* going on." He laughed and turned his back to me again. "Fuck off. I'll see, alright? But I'm not making any promises." He shook his head. "Yeah. Just like you. Whatever. I gotta go. Unlike you, I'm actually working. Yeah, yeah. I'll believe it when I see it."

Then he laughed again and hung up.

When he turned back to me, his eyes emanated the calm warmth he only ever got from his family. They brought out this deep joy in him that made him shine. I didn't understand that feeling at all— not from family, not from anyone—but I hoped maybe someday I'd feel it too, and that maybe I'd be the one to make Dare look like that.

"That was my brother Dash," he said. "His band's on tour this summer."

"In Europe?"

He nodded. "We're supposed to hook up at some point, so he was calling to see if I'd meet him in Amsterdam. I just gotta get through this show first before I can think about leaving." He looked at me thoughtfully. "See what happens with…the art."

I busied myself with my belt, not wanting to think about Dare leaving just when I'd finally found him again. "When are Dalia and Dax coming?"

"I have to pick them up from the airport on Monday night." He didn't ask me to come along. And I'd be lying if I said that didn't hurt a little, too.

But I wasn't family. And he wasn't sure. And it was fine. Well, fine-*ish*.

At least that was what I kept telling myself.

Besides, the show opened Tuesday night and it would give me extra time to prepare for Dare's debut. And I could probably use the night off to see Archer again. He'd texted me a couple of times, but I kept giving him noncommittal answers to his invites to play. Now I could make a solid plan with him, which would be good.

Things were coming together. *Finally.*

My life no longer felt out of control.

eighteen

"You sure you don't want to go out?" Archer said as he eyed my apartment from the doorway. "I'll take you someplace nice. Like over in the eighth *arrondissement*."

"I'd rather eat in." I walked into the kitchen.

He raised a very skeptical eyebrow at me. "Really?"

"Don't worry, Arch. I'm not cooking. I haven't fallen *that* far." Not that I didn't want to learn how, but I knew Archer wouldn't really understand that. I pulled a couple of plates out of the cupboard as he laughed. "I picked up some takeout from a couple of local restaurants."

He wandered into the living room and dropped down onto the couch. "So where is he?"

"Dare?" I didn't have to ask. I knew who he was talking about. "He's doing a final check at the gallery for his show, then he's going to pick up his brother and sister at the airport."

"Christ. Do people actually do that?" Archer shook his head. "Meet each other at airports? That's so quaint. I wouldn't pick up *my* brother at an airport."

I laughed. "That's because you absolutely loathe Spencer."

"Yeah." He smirked. "True."

"Dare likes his siblings. Loves them to pieces actually."

Archer's icy eyes widened as he shook his head. "I can't even fathom that. I wonder what it's like."

I rolled my eyes and threw a napkin at him which he easily caught. "You'd meet me at an airport, wouldn't you? If I asked?"

He shrugged. "It would depend on what I was doing. Or, more likely, *who* I was doing." When I put my hands on my hips and gave him my trademark *Archer-is-being-an-ass-AGAIN* stare, he laughed. "I'd send a car for you at the very least."

"That's just so...*something*."

"Well, you are my best friend." He grinned as I brought the food over and set it on the coffee table.

I lit a couple of candles and placed them on the table between us. "For atmosphere," I said, sitting down on the floor opposite of him. "I didn't want you to miss out on all the fancy things you're used to just because we're eating in."

He was silent for a while before saying, "I've missed you, baby girl. Things just aren't the same without you around. When are you coming home?"

I shook my head as I handed him a plate. "If I can help it, never."

"Reagan! Seriously? What about Harvard? Your law degree? We'll be there together."

"I don't want it, Archer. None of it. I never have. It just took me this long to finally say so." I waved my hand at the apartment. "I *love* it here. Like LOVE love. It's fucking amazing to be actually doing something I care about, something that's important to me." I lifted my wine glass at him. "You should try it sometime. It's addictive."

"So is money."

"True," I said. "But that addiction can be broken. This one can't." Nor could my addiction to Dare. But I wasn't going to say that to Archer.

A knock sounded at the door, but before I could get up to answer it, it swung open.

"Is she here? Where is she? Ree!" A vaguely familiar female voice called out.

Dare appeared in the entryway and froze at the sight of Archer and me.

I hadn't told him we were getting together, and

I suddenly realized how this probably looked to him—candlelight, wine, dinner alone. Not good. Pretty bad, in fact. Maybe even fucking awful, but it was innocent. He *had* to know that.

"Dare, get out of the way!"

He stepped aside, wincing as Dalia pushed her way into the room. She tackled me to the ground with a hard hug.

"Oh my god," she said, leaning back for a second to look at me. "I can't believe it! It's really you! In the flesh!" She embraced me tightly again, and I squeezed right back. It felt so good. I'd forgotten how wonderful it felt to be hugged. I inhaled, taking in a deep breath of her. She smelled like soap and sunshine. And love. Dalia always smelled like love.

I pulled away to get a good look at her myself. Three years had changed her. Where before she'd been a pretty girl, at nineteen she was stunningly beautiful—long dark hair hung in waves past her shoulders, she had strong sculpted arms that I couldn't help but envy, and her eyes were the same amber as her twin brother's.

"Reagan, you're even more of a babe than before." Dax grinned, standing over us both, holding a hand out to help me up. His dark hair stood in the same spiky mess, but the rest of him had changed. He'd filled out since I'd last seen him, and grown at least four inches which I really noticed when he crushed me in a bear hug.

"Okay, okay," Dare said, peeling Dax off of me, "that's enough. She's taken, Dax. I told you that already."

Dax laughed. "Well, let's give her a chance. Maybe now that she's seen me she'll change her mind about you."

"In your dreams, Dax." Dalia hit him, which only made him laugh harder. I smiled so huge at them that my face began to ache. I'd had no idea how much I missed all of them until they were right here in front of me.

Archer had gotten up off the couch, and come around to me. He looked like he didn't understand the language the three siblings were speaking.

"This is what it's like," I said.

He nodded like he was unsure of it all. "I think I'm gonna get out of your way," he said. And when I opened my mouth to protest, he added, "Looks like you've got your hands full. I'll catch up with you tomorrow, okay?"

I glanced at Dare. "Dare's show opens tomorrow...so..."

Archer held up his hands. "No, that's fine. Just...let me know when you're free because I really need to talk to you about something important." Then he gave me a quick kiss on the cheek and left.

Dare had watched our little interaction, and I could tell he didn't like what he saw. I reached for his hand, and although his fingers laced through mine, his grip felt stiff and rigid.

So I pointed Dax and Dalia toward the table. "We have more food here than we can possibly eat, why don't you two help yourselves while your brother and I chat for a minute." I pulled Dare toward my room.

As soon as we were inside and the door was closed, he tugged his hand free.

"What was *he* doing here?" he said.

"We were just having dinner," I said. "He came to Paris to see me and I've only seen him once because I've been so busy with my work and the modeling." His eyes darkened and I hurried on. "Which is what I've wanted to be doing, but since you were busy this afternoon and evening, I made plans," I said, placing my palms on his chest. "I forgot to tell you. That's all."

I took a step toward him, but he stepped back. So I just kept moving until he was backed up against the wall, my body tightly pressing against his.

"I'm yours, Dare Wilde," I said. "Completely yours. Don't ever doubt that. There is nothing going on between Archer and me. We had dinner tonight because we're good friends."

"Without any benefits?" His eyes narrowed, but a small smile tugged at the corners of his lips.

"You're the only one on my benefits plan." I pressed closer into him, feeling him hardening at the contact. "I promise."

"Good." He lowered his head to whisper against my mouth. "Because in order to enjoy all the wickedly delightful things I have planned for us, you'll have to be mine. All mine."

I was suddenly wet with want. "I am all yours." Taking hold of his hand, I guided it up under my dress, slid it over my stomach and down into my panties, opening my legs to let him feel me.

He groaned as he began to stroke me, his fingers slipping deep inside me, drawing moans from my lips.

"See?" I panted, my breaths short and quick as my body tingled from his touch. "That's all you. Just you. You made me like that." I kissed him hard on the mouth, pulling his bottom lip between my teeth. "Now," I said, staring into his deep, dark eyes, "I dare you to do something about it."

Fifteen minutes later, I was trying really hard

not to blush as we came back out of my room. We hadn't made a sound, but by the looks on their faces Dalia and Dax knew. Dare glared at Dax and took a swipe at the shit-eating grin on his face, but Dax dodged it easily. He lunged at Dare, crashing into him and tackling him to the ground, pinning Dare on his back.

"Not so much the little brother anymore, am I?" Dax said, laughing. He shook his head. "You've gotten soft in your old age, you know that, Dare?"

Dare tried to throw him off but couldn't, causing Dax to crow in triumph.

Dalia rolled her eyes, crossed her arms over her chest, and sank her weight into one hip. "Sometimes you two are such BOYS."

"Okay, okay," Dare said. "Get up."

Dax started to climb off of him, but Dare swung his leg up, knocking Dax forward, and wrestled him onto the ground, his knees digging into Dax's back.

"Hey!" Dax yelled. "I call foul. You gave up."

Dare leaned his face next to Dax's ear and said, "I don't ever give up, little bro. *Ever.*"

"But you said it!"

"I said *get up*, not *give up*. Clean out your ears." He smacked the back of Dax's head and leaned a little harder on his back as Dax grunted in pain. "I can't hear you saying *uncle*..."

"That's because I'm not—*OW!* Okay, okay. Uncle, asshole."

Dalia turned to me. "That is totally what Dax's future kids will call Dare. He'll be Uncle Asshole, I have no doubt."

Dare gave one last lean into Dax. "They better not," he said, and laughed. "And those future rug rats better not exist for a while. A *long* while." Then he got up and helped Dax to his feet.

Watching the three of them laugh and play around together filled me with happiness. They so clearly cared about each other in a way that ran deeper than just the blood that flowed through their veins. All the advantages of my life and privileged existence was worthless compared to what Dare and his family had.

And while I didn't totally understand this kind of family, I yearned for it.

It was like I'd spent a lifetime in withdrawal, and just a taste—a single glimpse—had me craving it like a drug.

nineteen

I was a nervous wreck as I approached the gallery. I'd spent the morning and early afternoon with my stomach in knots—equal parts excited and nervous for Dare. This show was huge. It could be his big break.

I'd taken extra care getting ready because I wanted everything to be perfect for him, including me. My dress was a deep blue vintage number that floated around me in soft silkiness. My hair hung down my back, long and straight. As always, my makeup was minimal—just eyeliner, mascara, and a touch of lip gloss.

I looked good. I felt good. And I was ready to cheer Dare on as he stood in his well-deserved spotlight.

Now, as I smoothed my hair, the butterflies in my stomach awoke. Everything felt monumental today—every little piece of this day was filled with purpose and meaning.

Okay. I needed to calm the fuck down.

I took a deep breath and headed for the gallery door.

"Ree!" Dalia and Dax were walking up the street from the other direction. I couldn't believe how good it felt to see them—I'd never felt this with any of my friends, never really missed any of them before. Other than Archer. And even that felt different than the feeling I got with the twins.

When I was with Dare and his family, I *belonged*—not in the same way that they belonged to each other, but I felt like I was welcome, that I was wanted and valued just for being me. It was heady stuff. I was pretty sure I was falling in love with the Wildes.

"You look gorgeous," Dalia said when they reached me. "That dress is amazing."

"Thanks," I said, actually blushing. Good god, who was I? "You both look fantastic."

Dalia beamed at me while Dax didn't even bother being coy about checking me out. I was just about to call him on it when the gallery door opened behind me.

"Eyes up, Dax," Dare said as he slid his arms around me from behind. I leaned into him as he breathed me in. "You smell so good," he said softly in my ear. "I could devour you right here.

Right now."

I turned my head so my lips were right next to his ear. "I dare you," I whispered.

His hands fisted in my dress and his chest vibrated with deep laughter, this incredibly happy, entirely free sound I hadn't heard in years. It melted my insides as I turned in his arms to look at him.

He reached up and touched my lips.

"You're smiling," he said. "I love it."

Me too. I never wanted to stop.

When I finally walked into the gallery, the surroundings took my breath away. There were beautiful nudes everywhere, years of paintings Dare had done as well as the new ones he'd just finished. I could see a progression of my facial expressions he'd captured over the past weeks—from bittersweet to yearning to lustful to content. He'd portrayed the beginning of our re-relationship on canvas.

But the biggest surprise was the nudes of me from three years ago—paintings he must have done from his sketches. I was everywhere, nearly filling the entire room. Other models were scattered in between like passing moments in Dare's life, but the installation was mostly focused on me.

I walked around the gallery, taking in one after another, my heart beating louder and faster with each painting. I hadn't realized it when I'd first come across the ones on display at Montmartre, but those were me too. I could see it now. Every one had been painted from memory, most of the early ones hiding my face in one way or another. Almost like Dare hadn't been able to look at me, even though he couldn't help but paint me.

In the middle of it all, her bright smile shining, was *Real Ree*. The very first painting Dare had ever done of me. The one that had not been at the show at La Période Bleue three years ago. Back then, I'd thought that Dare hadn't put it in the show because he hated me and had decided to destroy it, but it turned out he'd taken it with him when he left.

Oh, my god.

He'd taken ME with him.

I tore my gaze from his work and searched the room for Dare. He was all the way on the other side, standing with Dax and Dalia and one of the gallery owners, but his eyes were intent on me, watching me. I had a feeling he'd been watching me since I first walked in, wanting to gauge my reaction at this revelation. The evidence was up on the walls. He'd never stopped loving me. And it *was* love, I could see that so clearly, could feel it in my heart even though we'd never actually put that label on our feelings.

It felt real.

It made *me* feel real.

I loved him.

My god. I *loved* him so fucking much. And I couldn't wait to tell him.

Tonight. After his show.

An incredible, albeit unfamiliar feeling bloomed within my chest, filling me with so much light I was sure my feet would lift off the ground at any moment.

I stared at Dare, tears in my eyes, and held up two fingers. *Two parts.*

He held up one finger. *One whole.*

This was it.

This was the life I wanted.

This was where I belonged. With Dare. The man who had taught me to love.

A burst of strength flowed through my veins. I would fight for him no matter what happened. Because we needed to be together.

My life was my own. Dare was my future—not Harvard, not my parents, not my father's political career. Dare.

My phone rang, and I reached into my clutch to pull it out.

Mother.

Perfect fucking timing. She always knew how to shit on my parade. My heart pounded like I'd been caught in the act, which was stupid because she didn't have a clue as to what was coming, in how many ways my life was going to veer off from her manicured path.

It was my path now.

Mine and Dare's.

twenty

I ignored her call and a minute later she called again.

And again.

And again.

And it was starting to really piss me off. So the next time she called, I answered. Just to tell her to—

"Reagan!" Shit. She sounded too happy again. *Something* was going on, and I had no clue what, which made me feel helpless. She was the master at that.

Why the fuck had I answered the phone?

"What is it, Mother?" I snapped, turning to face the wall.

"Your father just finished a press conference."

"THAT's what you're calling me about? Seriously?" She was un-*fucking*-believable. "Did he finally tell everyone he's running for governor?"

"No, your father demurred again, and the people there were practically *begging* him to run. It is all going exactly as we planned." What a crock of shit. I was so glad to be out of it. "We just wished you and Archer could have been here to enjoy it with us. You should see the way the press is running after Quincy and Pierce. You would think we were celebrities! Some reporters are actually on their way to your hotel right now to get your reaction."

"What? My reaction? To what—the fact that he keeps saying he's not going to run? That's ridiculous. I'm not talking to the press." I walked toward a quiet corner, turning my back on everyone in the gallery. I couldn't believe they were sicking the press on me. A part of me felt like just outing my father, telling them he'd always planned to run and was just playing a game to garner more interest from the public. "What hotel did you send them to?"

"The George V, of course. Where Archer is right now. Are the two of you not there together?"

"Mother, I'm *living* in Paris. I'm not staying in a hotel." I was trying to stop my eyes from rolling back in my head until I realized I didn't have to— she couldn't see me anyway.

"Reagan Allison McKinley, you are the daughter

of the mayor of New York City, soon to be the daughter of the governor. You will conduct yourself as such. And by that I mean you will gather up your things and move into a suite at the George V. I will call to have it arranged for you. In the meantime, make yourself presentable. I hope you are not wearing that god-awful vintage clothing you love so much, and have done something with that flat hair of yours. We cannot have the press talking about how awful you look on your special day."

Now THAT was what my mother usually sounded like. It was almost a relief to hear it. Almost.

"My special day?" Did she know about Dare's show? Anything was possible with my parents. I shook my head. "I can't talk to the press. I already told you I'm not at the hotel." Even if I was, I wouldn't bother with them. That wasn't my life anymore. I was no longer my parents' lackey.

There was a long silence on the other end, before my mother spoke again. "Well, where in the world are you if not with Archer? He flew all the way to France for you. To—"

"I'm at an art gallery. If Archer's at the hotel, they can talk to him all they want. He gives better press." A freaking dog would give a better, more enthusiastic performance in front of the paparazzi than I ever could.

"Fine. Archer will just have to bring them to you," she said.

She wasn't getting it. So I tried to be clear. "Mother, I'm not talking to the press. I don't want to. I have nothing to say about the campaign. And I—"

"Alright, Reagan. Congratulations and remember to smile."

"Congratu—what? Mother? *Mother?*" But she'd hung up.

I stared at my phone. What the fuck was she congratulating me on? The woman was out of her mind. On-her-tenth-martini out of her mind.

I was about to call Archer to warn him, but when I looked up from my phone, he was getting out of a car in front of the gallery, surrounded by reporters and photographers.

What the—

My first instinct was to rush outside and keep the circus away from Dare and his debut into the art world. But then I realized that this kind of publicity might actually be a fantastic opportunity for him. If they came inside to talk to me, I could answer their questions and direct the attention onto Dare and his work, giving him greater exposure.

Perhaps this wasn't an entirely bad thing after

all.

Dare was staring out the window at Archer, his brows drawn together, his jaw firmly set. I began walking over toward him to explain what was happening as Archer opened the door and let the storm of reporters in. When they spotted me, they rushed over, blocking my path to Dare. I gave him a little helpless shrug and hoped my smile conveyed that I was going to handle this.

They made space for Archer to come stand by me as I waved Dare over, eager to introduce him and his work. Of course my parents were going to see this, but at this point I no longer cared. Maybe I would even give Dare a deliberate on-air kiss just to fuck with them. THAT would really make this all worthwhile.

But before Dare could move, a reporter called out, "Congratulations on your engagement, Miss McKinley! Have you and Mr. Chase set a date?"

As Archer smiled and put his arm around me, my eyes went straight to Dare's.

His gaze was black with anger, and the color had drained from his face as he glared at me, looking like I'd just betrayed him. Ripped his fucking heart from his chest and then stomped all over it. His eyes stayed locked on mine, and I started shaking my head, just slightly. This couldn't be happening.

"No," I said, my voice barely above a whisper. "No, *no*..." Dare thought it was true. *Why would he think it was true?*

Several reporters turned their heads to see who I was staring at so intensely.

"Do you know this man, Miss McKinley?"

"No, she doesn't," Dare said before I could answer, his expression carved from stone, his eyes blazing into mine. He shook his head. "Clearly, this will always be your world, Reagan. You will never be completely out of it...and I want no part of it."

Then he turned and stalked toward the door, Dax and Dalia hurrying behind him.

"No! Dare, wait!" I yelled, shrugging off Archer's arm, but Dare just kept going, didn't slow down, didn't even turn to look at me. Dalia glanced back once, her face filled with hurt, and then they were out the door.

The reporters were shouting out questions but I couldn't hear them. I was pushing to get through, but there were so many of them and they weren't getting out of my way. Microphones pushed into my face, flashes spotted my vision.

Someone grabbed my arm and I whipped around to find Archer holding onto me.

"Archer. Let. Go." My words came out in a snarl as I yanked on my arm, trying to free myself from his steely grip.

He plastered a plastic grin on for the press as he leaned down to me. "Just smile and nod, Reagan," he said through his too-white teeth. "Think about what it's going to look like if you go running after him. Appearance is everything."

Maybe to him and my parents, but not to me. Not anymore. Fuck appearance.

So I turned right to the closest camera, hoping *they* would be watching my every move.

"It's a LIE!" I said, my words laced with venom. "We are not engaged and we never will be. I love the man who just walked out of here, and I'm going after him." I narrowed my eyes as I peered straight into the camera. "And this is for my parents—stop fucking with my life. It's MY life now. Not yours. Never again yours."

Then I was pushing my way through the group of reporters. More questions were flung my way, but I kept running until I was at the door and bursting out onto the street.

But Dare was gone. There was no sign of him anywhere. Nor of Dax or Dalia.

My eyes searched the streets—there were no cabs. Fuck, they were still on strike. And walking was going to take far too long.

I glanced down the block at the metro stop.

It was that or lose him.

And I couldn't lose him. Not again. Not now,

after everything we'd been through.

Swallowing my fear, I ran toward the entrance and descended into the darkness. Dare was worth every obstacle. I had to get to him and explain.

I only hoped I'd get there in time.

twenty-one

GONE.

He was gone.

I waited for hours outside his apartment, banged on his door, sat with my back against the wall, staring out into the empty hallway all night long.

Déjà fucking *vu*.

There was no doubt about it; I was paying for the betrayal I'd committed three years ago. And my punishment was losing Dare over and over again.

My heart couldn't take it.

"I fought this time! Fought for you! Fought for us!" I screamed into the empty hallway.

"I TOOK THE FUCKING METRO." And the memory of being down there, even though it had been well-lit, made me shudder. I'd kept my eyes closed the entire ride, I'd been shaking and dizzy…but I'd done it. "Because…you're worth it, Dare. Because I love you."

But he didn't hear me.

No one heard me.

Somewhere around dawn, the door downstairs opened and I heard footsteps coming up the stairs. I scrambled to my feet. My heart stilled, then hammered against my ribcage.

Dare hadn't given up on me, on us. I knew he wouldn't. I knew he couldn't! I was so relieved that tears of joy sprang to my eyes.

And then Archer stepped into view and my entire world crashed around me.

My knees gave out, and I collapsed on the landing, sobs wracking me. Dare was gone. He was really gone. He didn't want me. He wouldn't even talk to me, let me explain.

Pain fractured my heart, spreading through my chest in jagged shards, making every breath a torturous agony. Archer's arms wrapped around me, but I shrugged him off.

I didn't want comfort. I wanted Dare.

But I'd lost him again.

No, my father had forced him away. He'd made me a pawn in his political game, announcing my supposed engagement rather than his bid for governor. It all suddenly made sense—Archer showing up here unannounced, my mother's phone calls—they'd planned this. My father had carefully calculated it, as he'd done with every single political or business move he ever made. This was my parents' way of showing me I could run, but I could never get away.

Oh, god. At this moment, I was pretty sure I could have strangled them both with my bare hands. Especially my father.

"How could he *do* this?" I growled the words.

"I don't know, baby girl. But I think it says something that he keeps leaving you."

I looked up Archer, anger running through me. "No, not Dare," I said. "My *father*. How could he make an announcement like this? How can he use my life like it's just some fucking toy?"

"Oh." He put his hand on my shoulder. "It's just the way he is, the way our world works. You know that. He's just doing what he thinks is best for you."

I closed my eyes and banged my head against the wall. Literally AND figuratively. "Are you seriously defending him? This doesn't piss you off? Because he used you, too, you know. Why the hell did you agree to play his little game, Arch?" My head throbbed, and I rubbed my temples with my fingers.

Archer lowered himself down next to me. "What do you want me to say? Maybe I don't see it as such a bad idea, Reagan."

I didn't even know how to reply to that. Archer had always been such a team player, going along with what his family—or mine—wanted. I guess I hadn't ever thought about how very invested he was into the whole lifestyle. Or maybe...me.

I opened my eyes and he was on one knee.

"No." I pressed my fingers harder against my head as I started shaking it.

He reached into his pocket, pulled something out.

"Archer, NO. I'm not kidding. Put that away."

He couldn't be serious. We'd never.... We were friends. Good friends. Sure, in moments of weakness we'd been known to default to fuck-buddies much like we relied on pills and booze for the mind-numbing bliss they provided, but that was *all*.

Archer was the only real friend I had in our completely fucked-up world. My rock. I cared deeply about him, but I didn't love him.

And fuck it all, he *had* to know that.

This couldn't be happening.

But he was kneeling in front of me opening a little velvet box, his ice blue eyes shining.

No, no...HELL, NO.

"Reagan Allison McKinley, will you marry me?"

"Archer Huntington Chase, are you fucking insane?" I said. "That's NOT my life. I don't want it. I don't love you, Arch." He winced, and I reached out toward him, guilt filtering in. "Not like that. I'm not *in love* with you—I never have been. And you *know* that. I love Dare."

Archer didn't get up. "Reagan, think about it. We're good together, you and me. We always have been." He took my hands and squeezed. "Besides, what can he give you? Nothing. He's got nothing but paint and brushes to offer you. His family legacy is a prison record. I can give you everything you've ever dreamed of, and more. In bed and out." He grinned wickedly for a moment, then gazed at me in earnest. "You and I come from the same world. We belong together, baby girl. I think *you* know *that*. Your parents are right about this. Say you'll marry me."

And that's when I saw Dare.

Over Archer's shoulder.

He was frozen on the stairs, his eyes piercing my soul, his look of betrayal shattering my heart.

And in an instant he was gone.

Again.

Reagan and Dare's story continues in...

untamed

episode 3: escaped artist

Untamed 3: Escaped Artist

Dare Wilde is out. The McKinley family has ruined his relationship with Reagan for the last time. He's in Amsterdam, staying with his rock star brother Dash, ready to move on with his life and get Ree out of his head.

Finally, and for good. Problem is, he loves her.

So when fate leads Reagan to his door again, the two must decide whether their new-found love is worth the risk. Because two fractured parts can't make a whole, and they must face the demons of Reagan's past if they are to have a future together.

A muse and her artist. A star-crossed love.

Will the past catch up to them…or have they finally escaped?

AVAILABLE NOW
All books in the series now available

Want to be emailed when Jen and Victoria release a new book?

Get on the Mailing List!

Enter your email address at either Jen's site (www.jmeyersbooks.com/the-list) or Victoria's (victoriagreenauthor.blogspot.ca), and you'll be the first to hear when new books are available. Your address will never be shared and you'll only get emailed when a book has been released or is newly available.

acknowledgements

Our biggest thanks, as always, goes to our editor, Stevan Knapp. He's a marvel with a red pen.

Special thanks to our early readers and reviewers for being so willing to post your reviews quickly and in many places. That's such a huge help to us! Extra squishy hugs to Jolene, Jena, and Justin. Also many heartfelt thanks to the bloggers and readers who have become so excited about this new series, taking Reagan and Dare into your hearts, and helping us spread the word. Your support and enthusiasm is incredible, and we cannot thank you enough. We love you guys!

And lastly, we thank *you* for reading our books. You're the reason we write.

about the authors

Jen Meyers grew up in Vermont, spent three years in Germany when she was a kid, and now lives in central New York. When she's not reading or writing, she's chasing after her four kids, playing outside, relishing the few quiet moments she gets with her husband, and forgetting to make dinner.

She is the author of the highly-rated Intangible series, a young adult contemporary fantasy, and numerous contemporary romance novels.

Visit Jen online at www.jmeyersbooks.com.

Victoria Green has a soft spot for unspoken love and second chances. A travel junkie at heart, she believes in true love, good chocolate, great films, and swoon-worthy books. She lives in Canada with her high school sweetheart (who's graduated to fiancé) and their pack of slightly crazy, but lovable puppies.

She is also the author of *Silver Heart*. When she's not writing hot and steamy romances, she writes Young Adult adventures under a different name.

Visit her online at victoriagreenauthor.blogspot.ca.

Made in the USA
Columbia, SC
02 March 2022